# Talk hard.

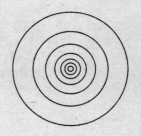

# Steal the air.

## PUMP UP THE Volume

A NOVEL BY

# J. S. Feliciano

A DELL BOOK

Published by
Dell Publishing
a division of
Bantam Doubleday Dell Publishing Group, Inc.
666 Fifth Avenue
New York, New York 10103

For Craig—
Happy Birthday

J.S.F.

# THE
# BEGINNING

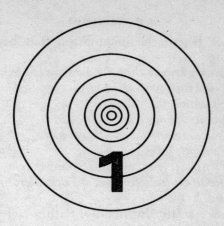

Nine fifty-nine P.M. A town in the desert. Outside, it is quiet, save for the throbbing chirp of crickets, a dog barking here, another answering there. Inside everywhere dishes are shelved, notebooks closed, TV's silenced, lights turned off, beds turned down. Everywhere the day is ending, preparing for another tomorrow, the same as yesterday and the day before.

⊙

Ten P.M. Time to invade the night, steal the air. A switch clicked. At 92FM, there was an electronic squeal followed by a hum. Then the familiar welcome sound as needle settled into groove. A gravelly voice began the incantation that began the beginning.

*"Everybody knows that the dice are loaded.*
*Everybody rolls with their fingers crossed."*
A voice joined the record.
*"Everybody knows the war is over.*
*Everybody knows the good guys lost.*
*"That's right, folks.*
*"That's how it goes, everybody knows.*
*"A little at-tit-tude for you all out there in white-bread land."*

He spoke softly, intimately, with a rich masculine voice that reached out one-on-one to anybody who was listening in Paradise Hills, Mesa, Arizona. It reached across an expanse of new homes, built to look the same, last the same, feel the same, hold the same, house the same. As the town expanded, so did the sameness. Everywhere, everything seemed the same, except at 92FM.

⊙

Holden Chu tucked his pen into its plastic case, turned off his calculator, switched off his desk lamp, and turned to his friend, Gordon Bilecki. They'd been working on their physics project together.

"Hey, do you want to hear something raw?" Holden asked with an intensity he usually reserved for quarks.

"Of course not," Gordon answered automatically.

Holden switched on the radio anyway, turning

the dial with surgical precision until the signal was clear.

*"And everybody knows that it's now or never.*
*Everybody knows that it's me or you."*

"That's him. The kid who has his own private radio station."

"How do you know?" Gordon challenged.

"That's his theme song. He broadcasts from his bedroom and calls himself Hard Harry because he has like this constant hard-on."

Gordon stopped entering numbers on the computer.

"We're practically the only people listening," Holden said.

⊙

Nora DiNiro lay on her back on her bed, telephone to her ear. Her room was her own, as different from the sameness of Paradise Hills as she could make it. Her walls were covered with her own artwork. The clothes she had designed and made for herself hung from pegs. The room was a cushion between her and the sameness of the world outside her window that threatened to engulf her. This was where she was safe and comfortable. This was where she was Nora.

Nora glanced at the digital clock on her bedside table. Ten-oh-one.

"Look, I've got to do my homework now. Call you later, okay?" She hung up the phone and switched on her radio.

*"Everybody knows that you live forever*
*When you've done a line or two.*

*Everybody knows.*"

The voice growled sensuously, cutting through to the deepest part of Nora, the part protected by her clothes and her art, by her own differences. The voice found the true Nora.

She stood up and walked to her window, brushing aside the hanged doll of Loretta Creswood, high school principal, as she went. She looked out over Mesa, wondering where Harry was, and who Harry was. This was the voice she allowed to invade her room and her world, coming in the night, every night, at ten P.M.

*"Everybody knows."*

"But nobody knows who you are, Creep."

☉

Mazz Mazzilli sat next to Joey at the wheel of his parked car, drinking beer and sharpening his knife. He had short-cropped bleached blond hair and four earrings in his right ear. Trouble was, he didn't like the taste of beer and he didn't know how to sharpen a knife, but he did know how to tune in a radio to Hard Harry.

*"Everybody knows the deal is rotten.*
*Old Black Joe still picking cotton."*

"You better believe it," Mazz said with feeling.

"So who *is* he anyway?" Joey asked. Mazz liked the feeling of being able to spread the word.

"He's nobody," Mazz said. "And everybody."

"How do you know he goes to Humphrey?"

"Just listen, man."

The song faded and the voice came back.

*"I was walking the hallowed halls today and I was thinking, 'Is there life after high school?' "*

Mazz snorted. "Just listen to this. He's right on."

*"And then I thought, 'Who the fuck cares because here it is September and I can't face tomorrow let alone the whole year. The more I think about it, the more I think high school is seriously warped. I don't care what anyone says."*

Joey nodded.

*"Of course, so's everything when you think about it."* The voice laughed sardonically. It paused. Then continued. *"Stay tuned, because tonight we have number twelve of 'One Hundred Things to Do With Your Body When You're Alone' as well as another semifinalist in my very popular 'True Pathetic Experience' Contest!"*

Static buzzed; interference on the air, another broadcast encroaching on Harry's airwaves. He whispered now.

*"Uh-oh, got to go. This is Hard Harry, saying 'Do your homework in the dark and eat your cereal with a fork.' "*

The air went dead.

2

Hubert H. Humphrey High School was a natural extension of Paradise Hills, Mesa, AZ. It was modern, made of light-colored stone, concrete and pale wood. The architect had described it as having clean lines. In fact, everything about it seemed to be clean. The 2,500 students who arrived every morning were neatly groomed teenagers, carrying unsullied books and wearing purposeful looks. It was Mr. Murdock's job to see to that.

"No flip-flops. You know better than that, Cory." Mr. Murdock pointed accusingly to Cory's feet.

"My shoes are in my locker, Mr. Murdock. Honest."

Mr. Murdock nodded and let him through. But he made a note on the pad on his clipboard.

The architect of HHH had unwittingly allowed

for a place the students called their own—the Alcove. It was an outdoor space at the back of the school, away from the principal's office, and the teachers' lounge. Because she could not think of a reason to forbid it or a way to control it, Mrs. Creswood permitted it. So the Alcove became the unofficial home of student cliques. It was where the Beautiful People and the Lunatic Fringe partied side by side. Portable radios and tape players blasted rock music that could barely be heard above the noise of the students' talking before the first bell.

Donald was open for business. He took a blank tape from Cory (now wearing regulation Reeboks), slipped it into the synchro-dub compartment of his boom box, pressed a button, and appeared relaxed. "I'm taping all the shows, but I missed a few when he first came on," he told Cory. "This is last night. I can supply you with any of them. Five dollars, please." The machine stopped. Donald took out Cory's tape and exchanged it for a bill. "Hard Harry has a really neat record collection and he plays these things nobody else can get on the radio." He rewound his own tape to his favorite selection from the night before.

"How long has he been broadcasting?" Cory asked.

"Last night was the fourteenth show," Donald said. "But he only lasted five minutes last night. The night before, he hung out for five hours!"

Donald pressed PLAY and began blasting a song he was sure would get attention.

"What's up?" another student asked, suddenly very curious.

"This guy," Donald said casually. He was about to hook a new customer.

"No music in undesignated areas, guys!" Mr. Murdock intruded. It occurred to Donald that he could point out to Mr. Murdock that he was only an inch outside the Alcove. He stifled the urge.

⊙

At the front of the school, Nora and her friend Janie approached. Janie's boyfriend trailed them.

"Oh, he's completely paranoid," Nora explained, "but I'm gradually collecting a whole file of clues on him—you know, things he says between the lines." Janie looked at her dubiously. "He disguises his voice electronically, so he could be *any* guy in this school. Want to bet I find out which one?"

Janie smirked. "You've got a crush on a voice."

"Not *a* voice. *The* voice," Nora said.

They entered the school. Two minutes to first bell.

Sometimes Nora thought the worst part of the day was walking past Mrs. Creswood's office. On her second day as principal, Mrs. Creswood had had a bench installed in the hallway to hold the line of students that invariably waited there for her to dole out her lectures, suspensions, and expulsions. The guilty students were lined up as a warning to others.

Mr. Murdock deposited Luis Chavez on the bench next to four other students.

"What are you in for?" Nora asked Luis, a quiet boy she often sat next to in her English class. He had recently moved to Arizona from Mexico and

was struggling with the difficulties of a new language, a new life. He seemed determined, though,
and Nora thought he'd probably come out all right.
Now he was on the bench. It was a bad sign.

"I walked on her precious lawn," he said, his
head hanging low.

Nora didn't have to ask who "her" was. "This
school is severely warped," Nora said.

"Hyper warped," Janie agreed.

⊙

Cory entered the drafting shop. First class would
begin in a few minutes. He spotted Eric's portable
tape deck. Without asking, he popped his new tape
in and cued it to Donald's favorite song.

Eric was about to get mad, but he listened, and a
leer crossed his face. Suddenly, other students were
listening. Nobody looked at the clock.

⊙

It was quiet outside the library. Donald could
open up shop again. Jack and Jim stood by as
Donald gave them a free sample.

*"I don't know what I hate more—that school or
the old bag running it. It's like she has a mission to
make that school unfit for human life."*

Jack and Jim listened with rapt attention.

*"Would someone please tell me what's wrong with
that woman? Besides the lobster up her—oh, well.*

*"Maybe some teachers are okay, but you've got to
think about what's wrong with a person that would
want to stay in high school their whole life! But the*

*true plague of their profession is the ambitious ones who climb up in the world and become ad-min-is-tra-tion."* He drew out the word in long syllables, holding it with his voice as if it were dirty laundry.

"Locker check! Locker check!" a student yelled down the hallway.

Donald pocketed his precious tape and flew to his own locker. Jack and Jim fled.

Mr. Murdock took a metal snip, clipped a lock, and began riffling through the locker with grim determination on his face. He emerged triumphant, holding a can of spray paint. With undue pleasure, he made another note on the pad on his clipboard.

☉

In the drafting shop classroom, students stood and listened to Cory's tape, oblivious to the banner at the back of the room that proclaimed:

**ONLY 200 DAYS TO SATs!**

The students were becoming as immune to Mrs. Creswood's campaign for success as she was to their burgeoning anger.

For Cory's part, the only thing he was aware of was how many people were listening to *his* tape. He was the center of attention—or was it Hard Harry's song. It didn't matter which it really was because everybody was standing in a circle around the two of them.

The shrill blast of a whistle cut through the music. In an instant the tape deck was abandoned as the students raced to their seats, leaving Hard

Harry's song blasting its obscene message. Mr. Murdock marched into classroom directly to the cassette player. He scanned the faces that watched him blankly, innocently. His hand found the button that silenced the tape. He confiscated the cassette player with its tape and turned to the students, whose faces told him nothing—and everything.

"I'm not stupid, you know," he said. He turned on his heel and marched out.

"Great imitation!" Cory muttered. The students exploded with laughter. Cory just loved it!

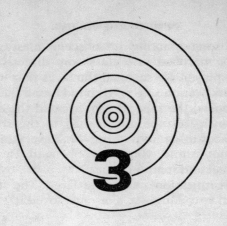

3

Cheryl Biggs sat outside Mr. Deaver's office. It wasn't comfortable sitting outside the guidance counselor's office, but, Cheryl acknowledged, being six months pregnant meant that almost nothing was comfortable. Stares, whispers, pitiful looks. It was all the same. Nothing could forgive her, except maybe she could forgive herself—with a little bit of help from her friends.

Mr. Deaver's door opened. He peered out. "Come on in, Cheryl," he said. "We must talk."

She knew he would talk, but would he listen? Wearily, she stood up and entered, ignoring the pursed lip glance of Mr. Murdock as he brushed by her.

⊙

Mrs. Creswood smiled broadly at her staff, which had gathered informally in the teachers' lounge for a last cup of coffee before the day began. She spoke to her teachers as to a captive audience bound by their contracts to listen to every word, and obey.

". . . and of course, in the end, a school is judged on one category only: academic scores." She smiled, almost waiting for applause. There was none. She continued. "The lesson of the eighties is that nothing good comes easily." The words came from her mouth easily, as if she had said them a thousand times before. "And of the nineties, it's 'no pain, no gain.' " She paused for polite laughter.

Instead, Jan Emerson, a new English teacher, spoke. "Yes, but the problem with back-to-basics teaching is that some kids—"

"A school *thrives* on standards, Jan." Mrs. Creswood did not like to be interrupted, particularly by anyone beginning with the word "but." She continued holding forth. "If it's too hot in the kitchen, then get out of the kitchen."

"No guts, no glory?" Jan asked wryly. Mrs. Creswood did not like to be mocked, either. They regarded each other carefully.

Murdock interrupted. "Third time this week," he said, slamming the purloined tape deck on the conference table in the lounge. He began playing the tape.

Mrs. Creswood's face remained stony while she listened. Jan hid a smile behind her coffee cup.

"Go to the beginning," Mrs. Creswood ordered. Murdock obeyed.

*"Would someone please tell me what's wrong with that woman? Besides the lobster up her—oh, well."*

Flushing bright red, Murdock slapped the stop button.

"That's all right. I know I'm not liked," Mrs. Creswood said in a tone that seemed to say she took pride in it. Her eyes scanned the table. Jan knew that something else was coming. Her distaste for Mrs. Creswood's iron rule had not gone unnoticed.

"Jan, when you've been around as long as I have, you learn that the student body can be divided into two categories: those that can help the school and those that won't." Behind them, through the open door, another door slammed. Jan and Mrs. Creswood turned to see Cheryl Biggs quickly exiting Mr. Deaver's office. She seemed to provide just the inspiration Mrs. Creswood needed to continue. "There are those who struggle and who will *always* struggle."

"Like me and my checkbook," Jan suggested, trying to lighten the lecture. It didn't work.

"The trick is to accept and accelerate the unavoidable—the inevitable. The students have choices. They can obey or disobey the rules. They know what the rules are. They know what the consequences are. The choices are their own. The consequences are, too."

Jan didn't remember learning this in graduate school. She looked around the room for help and found none. So, she smiled. Mrs. Creswood smiled back, satisfied.

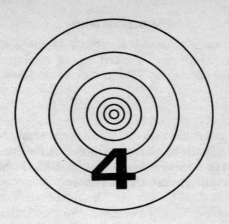

**4**

Ten P.M. Flip. Click. Buzz. Hummmm.

"Oh, dear, where's the . . . ? Ahh. Gotcha."

The iguana inched up the mike boom toward its dinner. It grasped the wriggling cricket in its mouth, taking it from human hands before the insect could flee again.

Human voice laughed softly, as human eyes watched the iguana devour its prey.

*"Everybody knows that the boat is leaking.*
*Everybody knows that the captain lied."*

Needles bounced on the Radio Shack transmitter. A homemade "On the Air" sign flickered feebly. The human hands adjusted knobs, turned down the music for the bridge, lined up tapes and records. The iguana settled down for the night, to digest.

"Okay, everybody, we got a list here: a boner, a

woodie, an erection—oh, that's boring—a throb-
ber—like that one, a hard-on, of course, named
after yours truly . . ." The music came back up.

⊙

Donald cued his tape. "Hard Harry Show Number
Nineteen. October first. Paradise Hills, Mesa, Arizona." He checked his wires. Satisfied that he'd
done it right, he sat back to listen.

⊙

Mazz leaned back and stretched his legs. He sang
along.
*"Everybody got this broken feeling*
*like their father or their dog just died."*
"Right on, man!"
Another car drew up next to Mazz's, overlooking
the school baseball field.
Janie leaned out the window and spoke to Mazz.
"Is this the place where the reception's the best?"
Mazz nodded. "He must live right around here,
huh?" Mazz shrugged. Janie tuned in her radio,
finding Harry's signal, then blasting it when it was
in synch with Mazz's radio.
*"I don't know. Ever get the feeling this whole coun-*
*try is, like, one inch away from saying, 'That's it.*
*Forget it!' You know the feeling—that something is*
*very deeply wrong and it's getting worse?"*
Mazz sat up. He knew the feeling. The voice was
saying what he'd tried to say, but the voice could
say it and he couldn't.
*"Ever get the feeling that everything is, like, disin-*

*tegrating? I mean everything. The food, the air, every-*
*thing? Or get the feeling that it doesn't matter? That*
*nothing matters? You could go out and kill somebody*
*and it wouldn't mean anything?"*

Mazz could feel the thrill welling up inside him.
It was there. There was an answer and the voice
knew it!

The voice belched.

Janie laughed.

*"You got it, folks. Hard Harry's on the rag tonight!"*

Mazz laughed.

⊙

Nora smiled. She picked up her notebook and
her pen. Harry could not hide from her for long.

*"As usual, I'm in a foul mood. But if you think I*
*have problems, I just heard they kicked out a senior*
*for being pregnant. It makes me gag to think of*
*Creswood kicking out kids just because they make her*
*cool school look bad.*

*"Yeah, she's supposed to be this new kind of 'nose*
*to the grindstone' principal, but I don't really get it.*
*Now I heard she's trying to outlaw heavy metal at the*
*dances. Says it's uncouth. So, here's Anthrax and*
*their latest contribution to the world's couth."*

The loud chords reverberated through Nora's
speaker, a welcome invader.

As the song played, she wrote "Anthrax" in her
notebook.

⊙

Paige Woodward's Bass Weejuns were by her bedside. Her Gap-socked feet were on her bed. Every-

thing in her room had a label, from her Laura Ashley wallpaper to her Ann Taylor wardrobe. Even Paige had a label: Perfect.

A Panasonic radio was propped by her mirror. She watched her perfect face while she brushed her perfect hair.

And she listened to his music.

"Hi, beautiful!" Paige's father said, entering without knocking.

She turned down the volume, but it was for her, not for him. She'd get a lecture if he could understand the lyrics. She didn't want to listen to a lecture. She wanted to listen to the radio.

"I don't know how you get such great grades when you listen to that all night." She shrugged. "Yale interview tomorrow," he reminded her. "I don't want you to look too sleepy." He smiled and left. Paige turned up the volume and considered the fact that, as usual, her father had hit the high spots of his emotional attachment to his daughter: her looks, her grades, her prestigious college. And he did it all within eight seconds, too.

⊙

Malcolm Kaiser sat at his computer terminal, cleaning his glasses, listening to the radio. His solemn face reflected the yellowish glim from the screen.

*"Sorry folks, but it's my biology experiment to think about sex twenty hours a day."*

The door to Malcolm's room cracked open. His mother peered in. "Finish your homework yet?" Mrs. Kaiser asked. Malcolm nodded in answer.

"Your father and I are watching TV. Why don't you come down and get out of your room for once?"

"No thanks," Malcolm responded automatically. The door closed. He was alone again.

*"Yessir, I admit it. I'm as horny as a ten-peckered owl!"*

⊙

*". . . ten-peckered owl,"* Nora wrote.

*"I swear, it's my affliction, my disease, my name! So be it!"*

"Insaniac!" Nora said affectionately to her radio. Then she glanced at her check-off chart. It was the HHH *Chronicle*'s center spread of all the new students in school this semester. Somewhere in that sea of the faces was the voice.

⊙

"What channel?" Cheryl spoke into the phone. She reached for her radio and tuned in.

"Ninety-one . . . two. There it is." She said "Thanks," hung up the phone, and listened.

*"Because guess what Cheryl's real problem is? Uh-huh. Right on. If she had good grades, they'd let her graduate. Cheryl. You listening?"*

She nodded.

*"Why don't you go over to the school tonight and just blow it up? Don't just sit around on your pregnant tush. Do something—even if it's wrong!"*

"What?" Cheryl asked. "What can I do?" There was no answer.

⊙

"—*even if it's wrong!*"

"Cheryl Biggs," Nora wrote.

"*I'm doing something. Can you guess what I'm doing?*" There was a wicked craziness in Harry's voice. Nora drew closer to the radio to listen.

A gentle, rhythmic sound. Thump, thump. Slow at first, then intensifying.

A smile crossed Nora's face. Was he?

⊙

Jamie's ears were glued to the radio.

"What's going on?" Janie asked, annoyed.

"*It,*" was all he said.

⊙

"He's not really doing it, is he?" Joey asked Mazz.

"A hell of a way to say 'fuck you' to the world, don't you think?" Mazz answered.

"*Oh, yes, yes!*"

⊙

"He's not, is he?" Paige asked herself in the mirror.

"*Oh, oh, oh!*"

"Really?" She turned up the volume.

⊙

"Listen to this!" Alissa said to her friend Sondra.

Sondra didn't get it. "Is there something wrong with the radio? I don't hear anything. Maybe the guy's in trouble."

Alissa shook her head. "Just listen," she said.

The rhythmic thumping increased. Faster and faster. There was heavy breathing.

"Really, he's in trouble!" Sondra said.

"Oh, shut up!" Alissa told her.

$\odot$

In a basement, not far from school, not far from the listeners, Mark Hunter sat alone, leaning forward in intense concentration, his breathing studied and loud. His hands were clasped, palm to palm, across one another, opening the closing rapidly, making a slight *pft* sound that was being broadcast throughout Paradise Hills, Mesa, AZ.

"Oh, my! Oh, my! Aoughhhhhh!" he cried out to the mike. Then there was silence except for the breathing, which he slowed to normal. Then he sighed deeply, contentedly.

"Yes, ladies and gentlemen, Hard Harry will go to any length to keep his three listeners glued to their radios! But the question is, How far will *you* go? Are you listening? Then listen to this!"

Mark cued his CD to a song that appropriately punctuated his show so far. He turned off his mike and took a break.

**5**

While the music reverberated through his studio, Mark danced. He grabbed the first thing that came to his hands, a putter, and it became his partner. It was slender and graceful, if rigid. But it didn't step on his toes—or require conversation.

He checked the disc. It was a long song. He had at least five minutes—plenty of time to grab a soda and follow a hunch. He unbolted his door and headed upstairs.

Keith and Marta Hunter were sitting in front of the television, talking. They didn't notice Mark as he danced into the kitchen and waltzed out with a soda.

"So, why *did* we move to Arizona?" Marta asked.

Mark paused. He had been wondering about that himself. They'd been perfectly happy living in New

England. He had been at a high school where faculty and staff sometimes showed some concern for students, where he had friends. He knew how his father would answer the question, though.

"Marta, we came out here because it's a nice place to live and because I get to be the youngest school commissioner in the history of the state."

"Keith, the man I married loved his work, not power and money."

Keith shrugged. "So, now I love my work *and* power and money."

Mark backed out of the hallway, toward the stairs, up to the second floor and into his father's office, his annoyance growing with every step. He slammed the door behind him.

In front of him, the desk was covered with papers. Mark shuffled through them. He knew he'd find something. He also knew that his protesting slam would bring his father upstairs. He found what he wanted and secreted the paper under his shirt.

"Mark?" his father asked, opening his own office door.

Mark looked up. "Uh, I was just looking for stamps," he stammered.

"In the top right-hand drawer," Keith said, reaching to open the drawer for Mark as if he couldn't figure out how to do it himself. "Planning to write one of your friends back east?" Keith asked with false cheer.

"No, Dad," Mark said, deadpan. "I'm sending away for an inflatable date."

Keith's smile faded fast. "Someday you're going to outsmart yourself, young man."

"I just love it when you call me 'young man,' "
Mark retorted.

"Look, you're never going to meet anybody sitting in your room. I bet that school has some really
dynamite clubs. It's very highly rated, you know."

"Great," Mark said, not giving an inch. "Look,
the deal is, I get decent grades, you leave me alone,
right?"

Before his father could answer, Mark brushed
past him and down the stairs. The five minutes
were almost up. His show had to go on, especially
now.

His microphone was waiting for him, welcoming
him, when he returned to his haven. He slid easily
into his own seat, patted his iguana, and prepared
himself for the rest of the show.

"Okay, folks, down to business," he told his microphone. "I've got my diet Pepsi." He snapped the
flip top. "I've got my cool French Gauloises Lites."
He lit a cigarette and blew out the smoke. "And
I've got that feeling."

He propped his feet up on the table and brought
the microphone to his lips. He whispered into it.

"I've got that old feeling that something rank is
going down out there." He sniffed the air. "I can
smell it. I can almost taste it. The rankness in the
air. It's running through that old pipeline out there.
It's trickling along that dumb concrete river. It's
coming *up* the drains."

His mind raced like an engine out of gear. But
nothing came that was rank. Every image he saw
was his parents, his own parents, trying to talk
themselves into being happy in Paradise Hills,
Mesa, AZ.

"I don't know," he told his mike. "I look around and everything seems sold out. My dad's sold out. My mom sold out years ago when she had me. They sold me out when they brought me here to this dumb hellhole. . . . Hey, how about this? They made me everything I am today, so naturally I hate them." Mark sat up. He'd thought of something rank. "Speaking of which, I'm running a contest on the best method to put them out of their misery."

⊙

Malcolm stared at his computer screen and listened blankly. His hands were poised motionless above the keyboard. Beads of sweat glistened on his forehead.

*"The winner gets my famous Lenny Bruce 'I Smoked the Toilet' Award."*

Fingers moved methodically. Words appeared on the screen.

SOLD OUT

THEY MADE ME

OUT OF THEIR MISERY.

⊙

Mark began pacing purposefully, carrying the microphone with him.

"Okay, so now we've finished with parents, let's move on to something ranker. The only thing I hate as much as principals is vice principals. But my pure, refined hatred is reserved for guidance counselors."

He retrieved the paper he'd stored in his shirt

and consulted it quickly to be sure he'd read it right in the first place. He had.

"I happen to have in my hands a copy of a memo written by one Mr. David Deaver, guidance counselor extraordinaire, to one Mrs. Loretta Creswood, a high school principal of your acquaintance."

He cleared his throat and read, " 'I find Cheryl is unremorseful about her unfortunate condition.' *Jesus*, he can't even say she's knocked up!"

⊙

Alone in her bedroom, Cheryl listened intently.

" *'And she is unwilling to minimize its effect on the morale of the student population.'*

*"Guidance counselors!"* An explosive raspberry blasted across the airwaves. *'Think of it. If they knew anything about career moves, would they have ended up as guidance counselors?"*

Cheryl laughed for the first time since she'd walked out of Deaver's office. It felt good.

"Bizarre," she said, understanding. And she didn't mean Harry.

Mark's eyes lit up. The gears engaged.

"What do you say we call Deaver up. See how remorseful *he* is."

He flipped through the pages of a directory he'd taken from his father's desk several days ago.

"Hard Harry just happens to have the home phone numbers of every employee of the Paradise Hills School Commission."

He picked up his cordless phone, clicked it on, and dialed.

*"Deaver residence."* It was him.

"Good evening, Mr. Deaver? You're on the air, sir, with Radio WKPX and we're doing a piece on high schools. I understand you're a guidance counselor?"

⊙

Deaver switched the phone from his right to left ear. He spoke into it.

"Yes, um, I'm head of guidance at Hubert Humphrey High here in—"

*"Could you tell us a bit about what you do?"* the voice asked.

"Well." He cleared his throat. "I run a comprehensive American values program for the young people at HHH in which we discuss, uh, ethical—"

*"So what do you say to 'young people' who look around and see that America has become, like, a sleazy country? You know, a country you can't trust?"*

Sleazy?

The voice went on.

*"Like your school. How come it wins all these awards and yet kids are dropping out like flies. Why is that?"*

It was a fake! Some kind of practical joke, he knew. But—

*"Before you hang up, Mr. Deaver, my listeners are wondering about your participation in the decision to expel Cheryl Biggs."*

Then all systems were on alert. Fake, maybe; joke, no.

"I really don't know what you're referring to," Deaver said, running for a cover of ignorance.

Then the voice began reading. His words. His

own words. They echoed rudely in his ear. Cold, uncaring, unfeeling.

"Who is this?" he demanded.

*"So, do you admit it?"*

"Admit what?"

*"That you're a slime!"*

It was a few seconds before Deaver could hang up. He listened.

*"You see, Mr. Deaver, when you interview a student and then rat on her, you betray her trust, right?"*

He could hang up then. He did.

⊙

Mark listened to the click and the empty hum that followed.

"Ah, well, as you can see, these guys are played out. Society's mutating so rapidly that anyone over the age of twenty really has no idea.

"Now comes our ever-popular 'Letters' segment. You guys are starting to write to me a lot. Weird. There *are* more than three of you—or else you're good at disguising your handwriting."

He shuffled through the small pile of letters, picked up a familiar one, and dealt with it quickly.

"To 'Confidential': See a doctor. Seriously. No joke. These are weird times. If you don't want to see your regular doctor, maybe you could go to an emergency room and give a phony name. I hope it works out. Let me know, okay?"

He tossed the letter aside and picked up another. The envelope was purple and flowered. The ink was perfumed.

" 'Dear Hard Harry,' " he read. " 'My boyfriend

won't talk to me anymore. He saw me talking to my girlfriend's brother,' blah-blah-blah. I don't know anything about these letters asking for 'love' advice. I mean, if I knew anything about love, I'd be out there *making* it instead of sitting in here talking to you guys.''

He dropped that one in the trash. "Okay, so send me stuff at Box 2710, USA–MAIL, Paradise Hills, Mesa, AZ. A reply is guaranteed.''

He picked another letter off the pile.

'' 'Dear Harry, I think you're boring and obnoxious and have a high opinion of yourself.' '' Harry chuckled. "Of course, some of you are thinking I sent that to myself.'' He continued. '' 'I think school is okay if you just look at it right. I like your music, but I really just don't see why you can't be cheerful for one second.' ''

Harry sat back and reflected. He pulled the microphone over and settled in comfortably. "Well, since you asked, I just arrived in this stupid suburb. I have no friends. I have no money, no car, no license. And if I had a license, all I could do is drive over to some mall and maybe, if I'm lucky, play some stupid video game or smoke a joint and get stupider. You see, honey, there's nothing to do anymore. Everything decent's been done. All the great themes have been used up. Turned into Theme Parks. And so I don't find it exactly 'cheerful' to be living in a totally, like, exhausted decade where there's nothing to look forward to and no one to look up to! . . . Whoa! *That* was deep!''

He pressed a button on his console, releasing a long, resounding, echoing, bellowing fart.

"Moving right along. Hmmm. Here's a letter

from somebody who says 'Every word of this is
true.' Well, I should hope so. I insist on it! 'I share
a room with my older brother. Nearly every night,
after he turns off his light, he comes over to my bed
and makes me watch him . . .' hmmm-hmmm-
hmmm. This is signed 'Screwed Up.' Well, dear
Screwed Up, first of all, who isn't screwed up when
you think about it. Anyway, you're not screwed up.
You're an unscrewed up reaction to a screwed up
situation. You see, feeling screwed up in a screwed
up place in a screwed up time does not mean you're
screwed up—if you get my drift. Now, as you know,
dear listeners, you cannot call me, but if you en-
close your number . . ."

He reached for the cordless phone again and
dialed the number on the letter. A girl answered.

*"Hello."*

"Hello, this is Mr. Hard-on. You're live!"

⊙

Alissa couldn't believe it. *He* was calling *her*. She
pointed frantically to her radio so Sondra would
turn it down and listen in on the phone with her.

*"Is this Miss Screwed Up?"*

"Yes," she said, trying very hard not to giggle.

*"So a couple of questions,"* the voice said. *"How
big is it? This 'thing' that you mentioned?"*

Sondra giggled. Alissa couldn't help herself. She
did, too.

⊙

Mark knew. He played it out anyway. "Well, is it
bigger than a baby's arm?" No answer. "You don't

want to tell me or you don't remember? Or maybe you made it up. Remember, my dear, I can smell a lie like a fart in a car." He disconnected.

"Too bad about that one, actually. You see, to me the real truth is always a bigger turn-on. And it doesn't have to be a big deal. It could be anything. . . . It could be the time a girl smiled at you and you knew in a split second that you had the chance to be brave and . . . you blew it."

Mark remembered. He remembered it a dozen times, a hundred. He wasn't brave. He couldn't be. He could only be alone. But that didn't mean he had to be so sincere.

"So send me the most pathetic moment in your life. The most anything, as long as it's real."

Time to change the subject. This was too close to home.

He took the next envelope. It was red. He knew what was in it. "And now all you regulars, here's our latest entry from the Eat Me Beat Me Lady!"

He ripped the envelope open. " 'Come in,' " he read.

" 'Every night you enter me like a criminal.

You break into my brain.

But you're no ordinary criminal.

You put your feet up and pop a diet Pepsi.' "

⊙

Nora lay on her back, listening, talking along, reaching out with her voice, her feelings, inviting the invasion.

"You start to party. You turn up my stereo.

Songs I never heard but I move anyway."

Her hand crept to her mouth, touched her lips, almost to silence them, but they spoke.

"You get me crazy, I say do it!

I don't care what, just do it.

Jam me, jack me, push me, pull me, talk hard!"

⊙

Mark controlled. It wasn't easy. With everyone else, the mike was enough distance. He was safe from them in this room, protected by the airwaves, the curtains, walls, windows, miles. But not with this girl. She came to him with her words.

" 'Talk hard.' " he said, controlling. "I like that. And I like the idea that a voice can go somewhere, uninvited, and just hang out." The way hers did, on her red writing paper.

"Like a dirty thought in a nice clean mind."

⊙

Nora smiled. "Ummm."

"Maybe a thought is like a virus. It can kill all the healthy thoughts and take over. That would be serious."

"That would be totally serious," Nora told the voice.

"I know all my horny listeners would like me to call up the Eat Me Beat Me Lady, but she never encloses her number . . ." The unasked question hung in the air.

"Tough luck, Creepoid," Nora told him. She had a better idea, anyway.

⊙

Mark tried to imagine this girl, this Eat Me Beat Me Lady.

"Yeah, she's like me," he said to the night airwaves. "A legend in her own mind. But you know something? I bet, in real life, she's not really that wild. Maybe in real life she's kind of shy—like so many of us. Briskly walking the halls, pretending to be distracted. Pretending—"

Yeah, if she's like that, she's a lot like me. Too much like me.

"Hey, lady, you really this cool?"

⊙

"Yeah," Nora said. "I am."

*"You listening out there tonight?"*

"I'm out here. I'm always out here."

*"It's funny, I feel like I know you and yet we'll never meet."*

"We'll see about that."

⊙

Mark spun his chair, dizzying himself, clearing his head, shifting gears.

"I don't know. Sex is out. Drugs are out. Politics are out. Spiritualism is out. Everything's on hold. We definitely need something new. I keep waiting for some new voice to come from somewhere. Someone who says, 'Hey, wait a minute, look around.' Someone to say 'What's wrong with this picture?'"

He reached for another letter. "Maybe this is it," he said, ripping open the envelope.

" 'Dear Hard Harry. Do you think I should kill myself?' "

It wasn't what he'd had in mind. "Great," he muttered. "And it's signed 'Serious.' Ah, but there's a number here."

He reached for the phone and punched in the digits. It rang.

⊙

Malcolm stared at the phone as blankly as he'd stared at his computer, listening to the rings as blankly as he'd listened to the radio. He reached for the phone.

"Hello,"

*"Hello, Serious?"*

"Yes."

*"You okay?"*

No.

*"I guess what I'm asking is how serious are you?"*

Very.

⊙

Mark felt pain in the silence. Or did he? Was this another "Screwed up?" giggling into a pillow. Making him look like a dork?

"How are you going to do it?" he challenged.

*"Shoot myself."*

"Right. Well, did you at least write a note?" Mark probed. "I mean you at least have a reason, don't you? I mean, I hope you're not one of those guys where nobody has a clue why they did it. That's why we need a note, pal."

*"I'm alone."*

Mark heard it, he knew it, he'd lived it.

"Well, we're all alone, you know. Listen, I went to school today and didn't talk to one person, not counting teachers." ·

He was leaving. Mark could feel him leaving even before he spoke.

*"I have to go now."*

"Hey, maybe it's okay to be alone," Mark said quickly, softly. What if the guy was for real? "Hell, I'm always alone. I eat my lunch alone every day in on the stairs, reading a book. What about you?"

Click. He couldn't hold him. Serious was gone.

Mark pressed re-dial. Busy. He couldn't get through.

"Death, the ultimate trip. Cheap and easy to arrange. All you need is your life and a tall building. If you can *find* one out here!"

A joke, a joke. Was that all right? Would that reach? Was he listening? Could it cut through the busy signal. *Bzzp-bzzp-bzzp.* Again.

Mark was exhausted. Time to stop.

"I think I'll cut it short tonight. Got an exam tomorrow. Got to figure out what a cosine is. Anyway, so be it. Talk hard, show hard, and so on and so on and so forth."

⊙

"So be it and be it so," Donald told his radio. *"Good night, friends."*

⊙

"Good night, Harry, my man," Mazz said to his dashboard.

*"Join me tomorrow same time and, hopefully, same channel."*

⊙

Nora reached for her pad. "Math exam," she wrote. "Eats lunch on stairs."

*"It's funny. People always think they know who a person is, but they're always wrong."*

"I know who you are," Nora told the voice.

⊙

Mark couldn't turn it off. He wanted to, but there was something else to be said. Could he find the words?

"Even our parents have no idea who we are. Mine had me tested just because I sit alone in my room all day."

Pause.

"Naked."

No more jokes. "It always bugs me that everybody thinks they know who you are and who you should be. Who *cares* who I am. In real life, I'm probably just that anonymous nerd sitting next to you in chem lab. That pathetic human staring at you so hard. You think, 'How pathetic,' and so you look away and never look at me again." That was it. He'd said it. "So, sleep tight, Cheryl, Miss Cheer-

ful, Screwed Up. Good night, Miss Jam Me Jack
Me.''

⊙

Malcolm's fingers moved on the keyboard once
again.

NOBODY HAS A CLUE

SO BE IT

*"Sleep tight, Mr. Serious. Maybe you'll feel better
tomorrow."*

Click. Hummm.

# THE MIDDLE

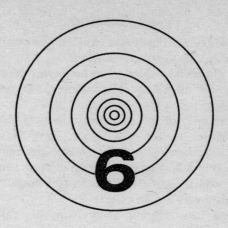

**6**

Mark held his books close to him as he walked to school. They shielded him. He adjusted his glasses awkwardly, tucked in a stray shirttail, and turned into the grounds, following the concrete walkway.

There, on the concrete walk in front of him, were the spray-painted words

## SO BE IT

He glanced around. Nobody was looking. He smiled.

Then he found more. Students on a stairway were listening to a tape of his broadcast. On the bulletin board, a fan had hung a banner:

# THE TRUTH IS A VIRUS

A student he'd never seen before was exchanging a tape of his show for five dollars.

Mark glanced at himself as he passed a reflective window. He didn't see Hard Harry. He saw Mark Hunter.

Mark Hunter didn't talk dirty the way Harry did. Mark Hunter didn't talk at all. Hard Harry was comfortable behind a mike. Mark Hunter wasn't comfortable anywhere. He grimaced at the reflection. It was a distortion like a fun-house mirror. Everything was a distortion.

He fled into school, away from his reflection, away from Harry.

He made his way to the library and silently offered his overdue book to the pretty dark-haired girl behind the desk.

"Hi, you're in my English class, right?" she asked.

"Yeah," he forced out.

She looked at him closely. He felt hot.

"I like Miss Emerson. She's pretty funky."

Mark stared at the desk. He couldn't lift his eyes anymore. He just pushed the book toward her. She picked it up and took it over to the card box.

"Big criminal," she said. "Now you're in trouble."

*She knows!*

She turned back to him, smiling. "You owe twenty-five cents."

*She doesn't know.*

He took a quarter out of his pocket and put it on the counter for her, then cringed as she looked curiously at the book she was holding.

"*How to Talk Dirty and Influence People* by Lenny Bruce," she read. "Who's he? Any good?"

No words came. He felt that awful feeling again. It was the one where he had a chance to be brave. He was going to blow it. He knew it. He blew it.

"Pretty good," he mumbled, and then he was gone.

He was gone so fast that he never saw Nora take her double spread of all the new students. She mused, locating Mark Hunter's picture. She circled it. Then, recalling his conversation, she put a big X through it.

"Cute, but *no* way," she said.

⊙

Mark sat in Creative Writing, hating the attention. Miss Emerson was reading his story. Students looked at him curiously. He stared at the floor studiously.

"Now, this is what I mean by writing with your heart and not your mind," Miss Emerson said. "Nice work, Mark. Do you have any comments to make about it? Would you like to tell us what you were thinking when you wrote this?"

Everybody looked. Everybody waited "Uh, I wrote it late at night," he said.

Miss Emerson laughed easily. "I realize that," she said. "It's practically illegible. But I was wondering if you could share your feelings about it with the class."

No. No, he couldn't. No way. No words, no language, no feelings.

The bell rang.

"Saved by the bell," Miss Emerson said. Students raced for the door. Mark tried to join the crowd. Miss Emerson stopped him. "You're good, Mark. You've got something. Beware of that."

He nodded. It wasn't that he wasn't grateful for her compliments, it was that he couldn't say anything. He was too unprotected, too vulnerable. He could talk to his microphone, he could talk with his pen. He just couldn't talk with his voice.

"See you later in Lit.," she said, excusing him. He left.

$\odot$

At lunchtime, Mark passed the Alcove, only to find his interview with Deaver from the night before, blasting out. Students were laughing broadly. If only they knew who Harry is, he thought.

$\odot$

Nora combed the stairways until she found him. There he was, the guy with the book. It was the same one she'd seen in the library that morning. He was new, he was eating alone on the stairways, he was reading a book. Next to him lay a pack of Gauloises Lites.

Bingo, maybe.

She stood in front of him until he looked up at her. She took a deep breath and spoke. "Are you really as horny as a ten-peckered owl?"

His blank look told her nothing. She didn't really expect it to. He would have to keep playing his game. She'd just play it with him.

"My name's Nora. What's yours?"

He slowly raised his eyes from the pages of his book. "Mark."

"Well, hi, Mark," she said. "Listen, I'm cutting fourth period. Want to join me for a smoke in the art room?"

He stared at her. It wasn't a leer. It was as if he were completely tongue-tied. Nora expected as much. After all, she'd found him out and that was the last thing he must have expected.

"Uh, no, thanks," he muttered. "Sorry, got to go."

She stood aside as he hurried down the steps. That wasn't what she'd expected.

"Hey, like I'm sorry, too. I thought maybe you were somebody cool."

⊙

Lunch. Mark hated lunch. Everywhere he turned, students were talking to one another easily, comfortably. And now somebody wanted to talk to him. Trouble was, she'd expect him to talk back and it was the one thing he couldn't do. He hid in the shadows until the bell rang for the end of lunch. That meant Lit. Class was beginning. He was okay in Lit., as long as Miss Emerson didn't ask him to talk.

He shuffled into the classroom and took his usual seat.

The minute Miss Emerson walked in, though, Mark knew something was wrong.

"Settle down, please," she said, her face pinched and pale.

The students became quiet.

"Last night, one of our students took his own life."

*Serious.*

"His name was Malcolm Kaiser. For those of you who knew him, there will be a memorial service at Dempsey Hall on Friday, and school will be providing counseling in the guidance offices during school hours."

Miss Emerson looked at the papers she'd brought into the classroom with her. She shook her head.

"I don't really feel like American Literature today, so why don't we just bag it. I'll give you the choice of going somewhere to write about your feelings or hanging out here with me and just talking."

Mark left.

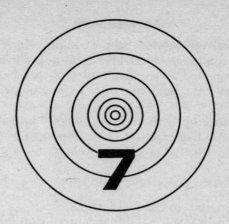

**7**

Nora spotted him from the window of the art room.
She stubbed out her cigarette, grabbed her purse,
and raced out the door. Everywhere students were
milling, talking intensely in tight groups. Nora
darted through the groups, following Mark Hunter's path away from school.

He walked toward town without looking around
or behind him. Nora kept half a block back. He
never saw her at all. In fact, she thought he looked
as if he hadn't seen anything.

When he got to the main street, he paused at the
light, took off his wire-rim glasses, and put on some
sunglasses.

Nora held back. Mark crossed the street and
walked into USA-MAIL. If she had had any doubt
before, she had none now. This was Harry.

She waited outside, out of sight. He glanced around the office furtively, took a key from his pocket, opened Box 2710, and took out his mail. Nora saw him hold her own red envelope in his hand.

Mark tore open the red envelope. Could the Eat Me Beat Me Lady speak to him, comfort him today? He read.

> *You're the voice*
>
> Crying out in this wilderness.
> You're the voice the makes my brain burn
> and my guts go gooey.
>
> Yeah, you gut me. My insides spill on your altar and tell the future. My steaming gleaming guts spell out your nature.

Mark leaned up against a concrete column. She had this way of reaching him. Her words always took him by surprise.

> I *know* you. Not your name, but your game.
> I know the true you. Come to me. Or I'll come to you.

"So you are him." It was Nora, the girl who suspected, the one who'd found him on the stairs. He'd been caught, found out, trapped. It was just a joke, anyway. Who cared? He cared.

"Don't worry. I'm not going to bust you or anything."

Mark wanted to talk. It was worse than before,

though. She knew his secret. He couldn't share anything else with her.

"Aren't you going to ask who I am?"

"Uh. No," he managed, smiling a little.

"I'm the Eat Me Beat Me Lady. You don't believe me?

"I know you. Not your name, but your game.

I know the true you."

She smiled at him.

"Come to me, or I'll come to

you."

Again she'd reached him, but this time it was for real. He was at once engulfed by his feelings and abandoned by his voice.

"Relax, I'm not like that." She smiled again. The smile that froze him. "Except when I am."

He spoke. "I can't handle this." He walked around her, heading for home, heading for safety.

"Hey, I'm sorry. Are you all right? Look, I was listening last night. I never thought he'd go through with it. Christ, I hope they don't blame it on you!"

He ran.

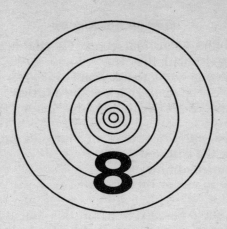

**8**

Nine fifty-eight, P.M. Mark glared at the television set. The oily presence and unctuous voice of Shep Sheppard Reporting, as if Reporting were his last name, intruded on Mark's studio. Good old Shep stood in front of a funeral parlor where Malcolm Kaiser's remains were boxed and people he never knew were crying.

". . . and so family and friends of Malcolm Kaiser sadly come and go into the night, even as phantom DJ 'Hard Harry' prepares to broadcast anonymously from somewhere in this formerly peaceful community. This is Shep Sheppard Reporting, Live from Paradise Hills. Back to you, Bill."

As if it were all Mark's fault. Just who was crazy here? Mark asked himself. He was alive, Malcolm was dead. So why had his own parents just asked him if he wanted to go to a shrink? He wasn't the one who decided to be the youngest commissioner in the state of Arizona, moving his son to a school run by a paranoid former SS officer. He wasn't the one who'd killed himself. He wasn't the one standing in front of a funeral home, telling the world his last name was Reporting.

Mark shook his head, took a tape out of the rack, cued it, and played a song for himself. Just for himself.

When it was over, he flipped a switch. Harry had something to say.

"You see, I never planned it like this," he began. "My dumb dad got me this shortwave radio set so I could talk to my friends back east. But I couldn't reach anybody, so I just started talking to nobody. I imagined nobody listening. Or maybe I imagined that *one* person out there who—" He saw Nora in his mind's eye. "Never mind. Anyway, one day I woke up and realized I was never going to be normal. So I said to myself, 'Why try?' I said 'So be it,' and Hard Harry was born.

"But I never wanted to hurt anyone.

"I never meant to hurt anyone.

"I'm sorry, Malcolm. I'm sorry that I never said 'Don't do it.' I'm sorry. I'm sorry."

He'd said what he wanted. He was done.

"Anyway, this is it. Show's over. I'm done. Stick a fork in me. This is Hard Harry saying 'Sayonara!' "

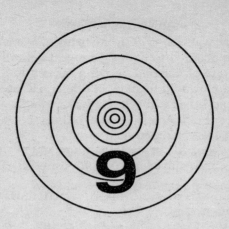

9

Nora sat up and stared at her radio, now silent.
"What? You're not quitting. Not *now*!"

⊙

Paige Woodward smiled. Count on Harry to be
funny just when you least expect it, she thought.
Then there was silence.
"This *is* a joke, right?" she asked her radio. Her
question was answered by its silence.

⊙

"Come on! You can't *do* this!" Mazz pounded at
his dashboard.

Nora was barefoot, but she didn't even notice the sharp stones in her family's driveway. She only noticed where it was she had parked her bicycle the last time she'd used it. It was there. She hopped on it and swerved down the driveway, picking up speed going down one of Paradise's hills.

She dropped the bike on Harry's back lawn and began tapping furiously on the window of his studio.

"It's me. I have to talk to you!" she said. He didn't move. She went on. "Look, you can't quit now. People *listen* to you! I know they're saying you're some freak, but you *know* you're not. I know you're not. *We* know you're not."

Mark turned up the music on his stereo, turned his back on her. As far as Nora was concerned, that wasn't good enough. She didn't know why he treated her so strangely, but she knew it didn't matter. What mattered was getting him back on the air. He treated her just fine on the air.

She slid open the door and entered, uninvited.

"Hey, I'm just trying to help."

As before, he didn't answer.

"Hey, don't you hear me talking to you?"

He stared at her, but he didn't talk. She'd had it. She'd delivered her message. She'd done everything she could. She wasn't going to stand there in his cluttered room like a fish out of water. She spun on her heel and exited the same way she'd entered, uninvited.

⊙

Mark watched Nora's retreat helplessly. He'd stumbled over his own tongue six times, trying to answer her, trying to explain, and nothing had come out. Now he tried again.

"Wait," he cried.

All he got in answer was the sound of her retreating bicycle.

He had something to say. He reached for his mike.

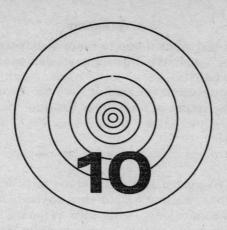

**10**

"You hear about some kid did something desperate, something stupid," Mark began. "What possessed him? How could he *do* such a senseless thing? . . . Well, it's quite simple actually."

Mark sat down. He took the mike off its boom, propped his feet on his desk, and spoke. He spoke to everyone who had ever hurt, everyone who had ever pained. He spoke to everyone who listened.

"Consider the life of a teenager. You have parents and teachers telling you what to do. You have magazines and TV and movies telling you what to do. But you *know* what you have to do. Your purpose, your *job*, is to get accepted, to get a cute girlfriend, to think up something great to do for the rest of your life.

"But what if you're confused and can't imagine a

career? And what if you're funny-looking and you can't get a girl? What if you have, like, pimples on your eyeballs!

"Nobody wants to hear it, but the simple fact is—being young is sometimes less fun than being dead."

⊙

Shep Sheppard Reporting stood outside the funeral home, waiting to interview anybody interesting who came along. He listened to the feed he was getting from his station, rebroadcasting Hard Harry's show.

"This is great," he said to his crewmen. "He's making it worse."

⊙

"Suicide is wrong, but the scary thing about it is how uncomplicated it seems. All that garbage swarming in your head and here's one simple—one incredibly simple solution.

"I'm just surprised it doesn't happen every day."

⊙

They heard him, all of them. All around the town, Harry's listeners tuned in. Donald pressed RECORD. Gordon and Holden left their physics project untouched. Cheryl clutched her enlarging belly, rubbed it comfortingly, and listened. Paige set down her hairbrush, Alissa put away her hot-pink nail polish. Mazz drew long sips of his beer. They listened. Jan Emerson, his English teacher, listened and heard. Mr. Deaver listened and did not hear. Nora listened and smiled. He had heard her.

⊙

"Of course they're going to say I said offing yourself is simple. But it's *not* simple. Like everything else, you've got to read the fine print.

"First of all, assuming there's a heaven, who'd ever want to *go* there? I mean, think about it. You're sitting up there on a cloud. It's cool—no parents, no high school. But guess what? . . . There's nothing to do. It's boring. Heaven makes Hell look like a place where you could at least not go out of your damn mind.

"Or maybe it's just black. Check this out. Just put your hands over your eyes for a little while. No. *Do* it. I'm doing it. Try it."

He slipped the mike back into the boom and covered his eyes.

"Let's do this for ten minutes. And then just imagine doing it for, like, ten thousand years.

"Boring, right?"

Mark picked up the mike again and stood up. He began pacing. "So, I don't know about you, but the way I look at it, Life is less boring than Death, which lasts a lot longer than high school.

"That's how I see it. So be it."

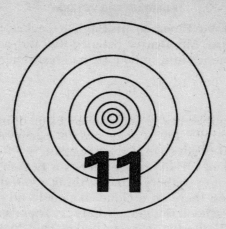

**11**

Four more cars pulled up near Mazz's on the base-ball field. All their radios were tuned to 92FM. The combined sound echoed across the field, carrying the message to the school building below.

*"And now they're saying I'm trying to 'counsel' kids without any training. Well, let's listen to what a trained counselor has to say for himself."*

There was a click and then came Mr. Deaver's too familiar voice.

*"I'm u-uh David uh Deaver and I really don't know anything, ah, yes, I'm ah-ah-aha, a, a, a— What is it? A guidance counselor in-in, yes, I'm u-uh David uh Deaver. . . ."*

Jeering laughter rose from the baseball field. Two students jumped out of their cars and began dancing wildly to the rap beat of the background music of their favorite new performer, David uh Deaver.

⊙

Mark smiled, listening to the result of his editing job. He'd done good work, somehow catching the essence of Mr. Deaver. He knew it was mean, but it was funny. His juices were flowing, his gears were engaged. It was going to be a good one tonight!

"And Deaver says I'm disturbed! He should check out his boss, Creswood—She-Wolf of the SS.

"There's an article in the *Chronicle,* the so-called student newspaper, calling me a 'garbage mouth' and a—let's see."—he picked up the paper and found the highlighted words—"a 'disturbed misfit.' "

"Could be, you know. I feel so strange sometimes. Let's say I'm watching a bunch of 'the beautiful people' hanging out in the Alcove. That smug, casual laugh. That smug way of moving. That smug way of wearing clothes with name labels in them. The Smugs!

"Everything seems too easy for you. Everything is a joke to you."

He remembered as he spoke. He'd tried to say hello to Paige Woodward one day. She'd looked at him oddly and walked on, trailed by three athletes. He'd blown it.

"I try to hate you, but the truth is, I'd probably love to be just like you. That's what makes hating you so complicated."

⊙

Paige listened. Was she a beautiful person? Was she smug? She didn't feel beautiful. She didn't even feel smug. She felt something else. Maybe he knew.

*"Anyway, I'm staring at the Smugs and I really must be crazy because suddenly I can see how incredibly worried they are. I can see it! In their clothes, their moves. And suddenly realize that every single kid in high school is worried sick!"*

He knew.

*"And I think, 'Am I the only one seeing this?' "*

"No."

*"Am I the only one thinking this?"*

"NO!"

⊙

Mark paced wildly, feeling the energy of the moment, the energy of his thoughts, the energy of his fears.

"How did I get so lucky?" he asked his microphone. He tossed the newspaper to his ceiling; it fluttered to the floor. He walked across it as he talked.

"Now they're saying I shouldn't even think stuff like this. They're saying that something's wrong with me and I should be ashamed or something. Well, I'm sick of being ashamed. Aren't you?"

⊙

"Sick to death!" Paige told her reflection in her mirror.

*"I don't mind being rejected and dejected, but I don't want to be ashamed about it."*

"Hallelujah!" Paige stood up.

*"I'd rather have pain than shame. At least pain is real. You look around and see nothing real; but pain, now that's real."*

Paige looked around her room to the pathetic unreal totalities of her life. Her cheerleading trophy, her dean's list commendations, her spelling bee ribbon, her Yale banner, her Macintosh instruction book, her string of graduated pearls.

*"Even this show isn't real. This isn't me! I'm using a voice disguiser. I'm a phony fuck. Just like my dad. Just like anybody! The real me is just as worried as anyone. The truth is, the truth is . . ."*

Paige ripped the Yale pennant off her wall and tossed it on her bed. She glared at it.

*"I don't know. They say I'm disturbed. Well, of course I'm disturbed. We're all disturbed. And if we're not, why not? Doesn't this blend of blindness and blandness make you want to do something crazy?"*

She took her natural hair bristle brush and threw it next to the Yale pennant.

*"Then why not? Do something crazy. Makes more sense than blowing your brains out. Yeah? Why not? Get creative! Get a load off!"*

Paige found the courage. She could do it. She could really, truly do what had to be done—something absolutely crazy. Something that would take much more courage than suicide. But what?

*"Got troubles? Flush 'em, chuck 'em, nuke 'em!"*

That was how. She tore down the commendations, the awards, the ribbons, added them to the pile on her bed. Her blow dryer, her electric razor, her tweezers . . .

*"Feel better! Save money on drugs and shrinks!"*

When she was satisfied with her booty, she picked up the pile and marched into the kitchen.

*"They think you're moody? Let them think you're nuts! Then they'll keep their damn distance."*

Paige stuffed everything she carried into her father's microwave. Then, as an afterthought, she removed her graduated pearls and tossed them in, too. She slammed the door shut.

*"They think you're upset? Let them think you might snap and go after them with your geometry set!"*

High. Two minutes. That ought to do it, Paige thought. Better than Defrost. *Start*. She walked to the other side of the kitchen table and sat. Waiting.

*"They think you got attitude? Show them some real attitude. Let them wish they'd never mentioned it!"*

The oven sparkled, crackled, and began popping. Smoke drifted lazily out of the top of it.

*"Go nuts. Get wild. Get weird."*

Paige sipped at a glass of milk. The oven rumbled.

*"Hey, yo! No more Mister Nice Guy!"*

The oven exploded in a glorious burst of bright white sparks and yellow flames, spurting pearls, trophies, and natural bristles everywhere.

Paige wasn't ashamed at all. She wasn't even afraid.

⊙

Mark howled. He held the microphone at arm's length and howled as loud as he could.

"Aoughhhhhh!"

It sounded good. It felt good. He did it again.

"Aoughhhhhh!"

He put on a record and howled with it, over it, along beside it. He danced and howled at the same time, working out all the pain, worry, shame.

"Aoughhhhhh!"

⊙

At the baseball field, doors slammed as Harry's listeners jumped out into the night, following the call of the wild, of the crazy, of the nuts, of their Harry. They danced, they screamed, they celebrated.

Paige returned to her room and listened, a contented smile on her face.

Everywhere, Harry's listeners felt his energy, heard his message, and understood. It was wild, it was crazy, it *was* nuts, but it was true, and it made them feel better to know that somebody else knew.

Everywhere, they danced, they sang, they yelled, they screamed:

"Aoughhhhhh!"

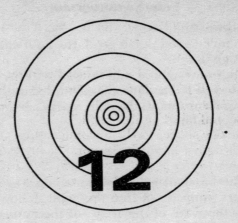

# 12

Mark finished dancing and sat down while the music continued. He shuffled through papers on his desk, vaguely aware of the needle bouncing as his signal continued feeding to his listeners everywhere.

He picked up a letter, opened it, scanned it. He leaned forward, turned down the rheostat, and picked up his mike.

"Time out," he said, still reading the letter. Then he reached for his phone and dialed.

*"Hullo?"*

"Hi, this is me. We're on the air," he said softly. "Are you willing to tell my listeners what you told me in this letter?"

There was silence.

"I think they're ready for it," Mark reassured the boy.

*"Okay."*

"Do you want to use the voice disguiser?"

*"No, I'm not ashamed. I won't be ashamed anymore. Like you said."*

"So, tell us what happened."

The boy spoke slowly, uncomfortably, at first.

*"This guy I liked," he began. "He invited me up to the ridge. I didn't really know why, but I was happy because he's pretty cool and an athlete and everything. I liked him, see, you know?"*

"I know. So, when did this happen, and how old are you?"

*"Just before school. I'm sixteen."*

"Go ahead."

*"We got up there and we took our shirts off and were fooling around and I sort of told him how much I liked him and he smiled and said he knew it."*

The boy paused. He was coming to the hard part. Mark waited quietly.

*"And then he said why don't we take our jeans off and get a suntan, and so I did. But he stalled."*

There was click in the boy's voice, the small gasp that sometimes comes with a painful memory. Mark knew. The boy went on.

*"Then two friends of his showed up and they were drinking beer and laughing and they threw my clothes in the trees."*

"Go ahead."

*"I didn't know what to do. I started to cry. But they laughed, so I stopped. They called me things. I don't usually care about that. I know I'm into guys, but*

*this was different. See, I didn't want* him *to be mad at me.''*

⊙

Shep Sheppard couldn't believe what he was hearing.

One of the techies, standing nearby, shook his head.

"Come on, Shep. He has a friend call in with some story they've concocted. It's not real."

Maybe. Maybe not. Then, "Who cares if it's real? People are riveted!"

⊙

"That's it. I'm calling the police!" Mr. Deaver announced to his wife. He picked up the phone. "It's fraud and pornography, to say nothing of slander. He's just exploiting these kids. *And* he's broadcasting illegally!"

He dialed.

⊙

"Yeah, right, we know," Officer Dennison said into the phone. "We're doing everything we can. In the meantime, why don't you change to another station?"

He hung up and turned to his partner. "That's the thirteenth call tonight," he said. "I heard some of it. Just sounds like kids playing pranks, don't you think?"

His partner shook his head. "I don't know, Den. Things like that happen when you're a kid."

Dennison regarded his partner dubiously.

"You're forgetting what it's like when you're young. You don't know what's going on."

"Pranks," Dennison said. "That's all."

⊙

Matt clutched the phone tightly, like a lifeline.

"I feel bad because I didn't do anything. I didn't even say anything. He won't talk to me now. He won't even look at me and I feel pretty confused."

Harry was there for him, on the other end, talking helping, helping him talk. It was good.

*"You're not the one who's confused. You sound like you know what's happening. Those guys are confused."*

Maybe. "I know that, but I just—" He couldn't say it. The words were locked in his throat. Then his own shame pushed them up and out. "I think about him a lot." He took a deep breath and cleansed his throat. "Sometimes I think everything's just a practical joke. Like the only proof that God exists is this joke he's played on us. . . . Like I wonder why one person is born one way and another person is born another way."

He waited for Harry to talk. There was only silence. Was it possible Harry was laughing—had left him, too?

"Are you still there?"

*"Yes,"* Harry said.

"I guess you think I'm a faggot wimp, huh?"

*"No,"* Harry said softly. *"I'm thinking how strong*

*people can be. And how everybody is exactly the same in a way. And how everybody needs the same thing. See, I didn't know that until now. I said it before, I just didn't know it before. Now I know it."*

"So, what are we going to do about it?" Matt asked.

*"I don't know,"* Harry said.

"That's the big question. . . . I got to go now. See you. And, thanks."

Matt hung up the phone. His hands were shaking and sweaty. It didn't matter, though. He was okay.

⊙

Mark let the silence hang in the air for a few seconds. There was nothing better to fill it with right then. The boy on the other end of the phone had filled the night with his pain. That was enough.

"I guess we all should go now. Good night, folks," he said, slipping a quiet song onto his turntable. He cued it and played it.

How could it be that something so simple, a homegrown radio station, could give him so much power? How could it be that people who were going to kill themselves wanted to talk to him? That somebody who had a terrible secret wanted to tell him—and everybody who was listening? How could those things be? How could it be that suddenly Hard Harry mattered? How could Mark Hunter matter, too?

It was Keith Hunter who wanted power. Mark didn't want power. He just wanted to talk. He didn't even care if anyone listened. Now everybody listened and they gave him power and he didn't know what the hell to do with it.

He turned the music down and took his mike off the boom. He wanted to talk again.

"I don't know. I must be losing it. This isn't fun anymore." He looked at his desk, his transmitter, tapes, records, CDs. He looked at Nora's letter.

"I feel completely afraid."

Click. Buzzzzzz.

**THE ENDING**

**T**he Pirate D.J. begins broadcasting:
"One day I woke up and realized I was
never gonna be normal. So I said
to myself, 'Why try?' I said, 'So be it,'
and Hard Harry was born."

All photographs by Joyce Randolph

**"I**t's funny," says Mark (Christian Slater) to the intriguing unknown Poetry Lady, "I feel I know you, yet we'll never meet."

**"W**e'll see about that," thinks Nora diNiro (Samantha Mathis) as she listens to Harry read her work.

**N**ora knows
the Pirate D.J.
goes to Hubert
Humphrey
High, and she's
determined to
find him.

**M**ark
eavesdrops as
students at
school talk
about his
show.

**"H**i, you're in my English class, right?"
says Nora at the returns desk.

**"T**he more
I think about
it, the more I
think high
school is
seriously
warped. I
don't care
what anyone
says."

**T**he clues
start to add up.

**G**otcha! "My name's Nora. What's yours?" *She knows!*

**S**tudents at school listen to the latest tape of Harry's show. Who *is* this guy?

**O**n the air: "You got troubles? Flush 'em. Chuck 'em. Nuke 'em."

**"I**'m sorry, Malcolm," says Mark, devastated when he learns Malcolm Kaiser is dead.

**N**ora listens to Mark on the air and feels his pain. He *can't* quit his show now!

"They say I'm deluded, demented, deranged; but guess what I say?"

"**I** got that old feeling that something *rank* is going down out there."

"This is Hard Harry sayin' 'Do your homework in the dark and eat your cereal with a fork.'"

**M**ark's parents (Scott Paulin and Mimi Kennedy) are relieved when they conclude he's not that crazy Pirate D.J....

. . . but little do they know!

**N**ora and Janie (Lala) survey the students' Wailing Wall. Harry's back on the air and the natives are getting restless.

**D**onald (Dan Eisenstein) and Joey (Seth Green) rig the school's P.A. system and out comes the voice of guidance counselor David Deaver.

"**W**hat is wrong with this school?" asks English teacher Jan Emerson (Ellen Greene) as she confronts Principal Creswood (Annie Ross) in front of the Wall.

**M**urdock (Andy Roman) collars Mazz Mazzilli (Billy Morrisette), but strong-arm tactics can't stop the students now.

"**I** have something to say to you people," cries Paige Woodward (Cheryl Pollak). Mrs. Creswood scowls at her.

**M**ark and his mother listen to Paige as the truth starts to come out.

The Feds are on to him—will Harry's show go on? Eager fans wait impatiently to find out.

The energy builds...and builds. Radios crackle. It's time. Time for Mark to talk hard—and be heard.

"**A**merica's ready for a million voices crying out in the wilderness of the suburbs! Feel the air. Keep the air alive. Starting NOW!"

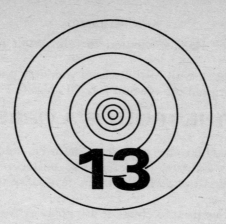

**13**

The sun shone down on Paradise Hills, Mesa, AZ, the next morning, just as it did almost every morning of the year. The growing town was the same as it had been yesterday and the day before—the same as it would be tomorrow.

But for Mark Hunter, nothing was the same. On the surface it was. He adjusted his glasses and shifted the weight of his backpack, walking quickly to school, dodging a backhoe that was building another house the same as the one next door. But underneath, nothing could ever be the same and the newspaper headline he spotted proved it to him.

# TEEN RADIO PIRATE UPS ATTACKS

Pirate? He just wanted to talk. What did they know?

The back wall of the school was now painted in international orange and Day-Glo pink:

# THE TRUTH IS A VIRUS

Everywhere he turned, something said, "Talk Hard." T-shirts, book covers, bulletin boards. Harry was everywhere. It was just Mark who was still alone.

Mark wanted to chuck it all, go away from it all. Then he passed Mr. Deaver's office. The determined guidance counselor was hanging a banner outside his own office. It read BIONIC, and underneath was an explanation. Believe It or Not, I Care, and there was a phone number.

Mark wanted to chuck it, but Harry still had a lot of work to do.

⊙

Mrs. Creswood's face was stony with anger.

"How's he getting this information?" she demanded from the staff gathered around her. Nobody had an answer. "I want a list of every student with relatives—"

Murdock entered the lounge. "Just found graffiti on the roof of the cafeteria," he said, explaining his tardiness. "They're taking it down now."

"What does it say?" Mrs. Creswood demanded.

Murdock demurred.

"Go ahead. I can take it," Mrs. Creswood promised.

"It says 'Creswood's a maggot pus-wad.' "

Mrs. Creswood stared. She dismissed the staff. Jan stayed behind.

"Can I ask you something?" Mrs. Creswood nodded impatiently. "Can you tell me why Luis Chavez was expelled?"

"We were having problems with him," Mrs. Creswood answered evasively.

"What kind of problems? He was making real progress in my class—picking up vocabulary like I couldn't believe."

"Well, he violated the school rules once too often."

"What rules in particular?" Jan asked.

"School discipline is not your concern, Miss Emerson," Mrs. Creswood said, closing the subject. Jan left quickly.

Murdock reappeared in Mrs. Creswood's office then, holding Donald's ear with one hand and his tape deck with the other.

"I caught him selling tapes of that Harry guy," Murdock announced proudly, as if he'd just made a major collar.

Donald was pushed into the chair across from Mrs. Creswood's desk.

"Who is he?" Murdock demanded.

"Nobody knows who he is!" Donald said, now frightened. Selling tapes and making a name for himself as the guy who had The Tapes was one thing. Facing Murdock's inquisition was another.

"We don't believe you, Donald," Mrs. Creswood said, ice in her voice.

"I swear! Nobody has any idea!"

Murdock crouched in front of Donald, his face a quarter of an inch away.

"Well, you have until the end of the day to *get* an idea." He pulled back.

"And don't forget, Donald, your file is under review."

Donald was dismissed.

He stumbled out of Creswood's office, stunned by the experience. It was one thing to listen to Harry rag about the principal and the administration. It was another to be a victim. He wasn't laughing anymore. He had a better idea.

⊙

Mazz pinned a message to the bulletin board in the Alcove for Harry. It was one of many for him there. His said, "Right on, my man!" It was written with feeling, as were the others.

The students gathered at the Alcove read the messages, felt the feelings, were aroused, excited, and enraged by them. And it was all right to be angry. It was only wrong to be ashamed, and they weren't—they were elated.

Harry's music from the nights before blasted out of a boom box. Students danced and screamed:

"Aoughhhhhh!"

Mrs. Creswood marched to the Alcove. Without pausing, she slammed the boom box, silencing the music, stunning the students.

"That's it for music in the Alcove," she announced. She picked up the boom box she'd silenced and then silenced it permanently by hurling it against the brick side of the school.

"And from now on, anyone caught defacing school property is expelled. Immediately. Permanently."

Behind her, a student hissed. She spun to find the culprit. Faces were mute. Again from behind, a hiss. She spun once more. Soon there was a chorus of hisses, all anonymous, as anonymous as Harry.

The color in her face rose. She was completely helpless against the rebellion. She breathed deeply, trying to control herself.

The PA cracked to life above her.

*"I'm u-uh David uh Deaver and I really don't know anything, ah, yes, I'm ah-ah-aha, a, a, a— What is it? A guidance counselor in—in, yes, I'm u-uh David uh Deaver. . . ."*

"What is that?" she stormed. Nobody answered her. She left all dignity behind and ran to her office. The voice of her guidance counselor kept blasting out as she ran.

"They've bypassed the amplifier. They're in the speaker system!" Mr. Stern explained when Mrs. Creswood burst into the administration offices.

"It won't stop!"

"Shut it off! Shut off the whole system!" Mrs. Creswood commanded.

"We can't," Mr. Stern said. "They've bypassed our controls."

"Then turn off the power. Shut down the whole school," she ordered.

That, they could do. Mr. Stern hurried to the utility room, found the knife switch that controlled the school, and sliced downward, cutting all power.

Lights flickered out and Mr. Deaver's absurd protestations ceased.

The last thing Mrs. Creswood heard before she slammed the door to her office was three juniors skipping down the darkened hallway, calling out, "Eat me! Beat me!"

It was what she feared most. Anarchy.

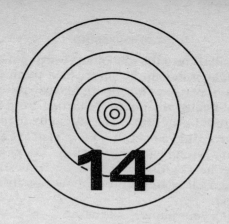

# 14

Mazz swaggered over to Shep Sheppard, who was busily giving his remote crew orders.

"You want to interview me?" he offered. "I was listening the first night he was on. I'm like amazing," Mazz said.

Shep Sheppard glanced at the bleached hair, the rip pattern in Mazz's blue jeans, his torn-off sleeves, and the four earrings he wore. He turned his attention back to his remote crew.

"I used to go here, you know, but they kicked me out for no reason. Know what I'm saying?" Mazz persisted. He couldn't get the reporter's attention. "Hey, look at this!" he said, lighting two smoke bombs. One white, one blue. "School colors, okay? Like it?"

Murdock grabbed Mazz by the shoulder and hauled him away. The last thing Mazz saw before being yanked into the school was Shep moving into the middle of the murky smoke he'd created, holding a microphone to his mouth and saying:

"This is Shep Sheppard Reporting from Hubert Humphrey High." Pause. Then he spoke to his crew. "Hey, guys, did you get the smoke? Isn't it great?"

"What's wrong with this picture?" Mazz asked.

Before he could answer his own question, he found himself sitting in a chair across from Mrs. Creswood.

"What's your name?" she asked.

"Mazz Mazzilli."

"Do you understand you're expelled, Mr. Mazzilli?"

He smirked. "That's cool," he said.

"I can quite legally expel you," she said, emphasizing.

"Yo. I'm already expelled. Don't you remember? You booted me out first week for violating your stupid dress code." Mazz pushed the chair back and stood up. "I told them cameras to wait," Mazz said to Mrs. Creswood. "I got lots to tell them about this place."

"And who's going to believe you?" she asked icily.

⊙

Mark wanted to get out of there. He hadn't meant to start something and now he didn't know how to finish it. He just wanted it to be over. He wanted to hide. He headed down the hall and walked toward the door as fast as he dared.

A hand reached out from the art-supply room

and grabbed his arm, pulling him through the door.

It was Nora.

"It's cool. We're safe in here," she said, the excitement sparkling in her eyes. "Guess what I heard."

He could look at her, but he couldn't talk. He wasn't safe with her. He wasn't safe anywhere. Words didn't come. They wouldn't. They never would.

Nora went on without him. "That tall Smug, Paige Woodward? She burned up all her stuff last night—right after you suggested it—you know, doing something crazy. It was in her *kitchen*. In the—get this—microwave."

Mark covered his face with his hands. It was too much.

"Her stupid pearls were flying like bullets! Her super dad was totally unthrilled."

"It's out of control, Nora," he said, speaking to her in a normal voice for the first time.

"Yeahhhh!" Nora said, thrilled. Mark looked at her. She didn't understand. She didn't understand about—the power. The dangers.

Lights flicked back on. The PA crackled to life.

*"School is closing for the remainder of the day,"* Mrs. Creswood announced. *"Students are requested to inform their parents of an emergency meeting of the PTA this evening in the auditorium. All faculty and staff are to stay behind for a meeting with the school commissioner."*

"That's it," Mark said to Nora. "The whole thing's over. I just hope it isn't too late."

*For what?* he asked himself as he walked off the school grounds toward home. *Just too late,* he answered.

**15**

The uniformed attendant behind the counter at the
USA-MAIL office held up one hand to protect his
eyes from the bright lights the remote crews of
three television stations had pointed at him. He
pushed microphones back with the other.

"Yes, of course that box was registered to a name,
but I can't give it out."

A brown-suited man with a narrow tie worked
his way to the front of the crowd.

"You can to *me*," he said, flashing a badge.

The clerk nodded. He consulted his list.

"That box is rented by a Mr. Charles U. Farley at
1122 Crescent."

"That's the address of the school!" one of the
radio reporters exclaimed.

"Yeah," said the badge holder. "And the owner is
Charles U. Farley. Chuck U. Farley."

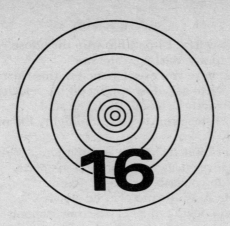

**16**

Mark took a bite of dinner. He had no idea what he was eating. He just chewed automatically so his parents wouldn't quiz him anymore about the things that were going on at school.

Keith Hunter glanced at his watch and switched on the television.

A reporter was standing in front of the high school and speaking.

"In our follow-up to Monday's suicide, we have the story of Paige Woodward, a senior at the same school. Apparently obeying the command of the pirate DJ to do something crazy, she destroyed her family's kitchen. Film at eleven."

Mark stared at a baked potato.

"Are you okay, Mark? You look awful," Marta asked, concerned.

"Don't worry. I won't blow up the house."

"Very funny, darling," she said.

"Mark, have you ever listened to this Harry character?" Keith asked, snapping off the television.

"Not exactly listened, Dad," he said.

"Well, I'm going to listen tonight, I'll promise you that."

"I don't think he's going on anymore," Mark said, shoving three peas to the edge of his plate.

"How do you know?" Marta asked.

Mark took a bite and chewed slowly.

"He's knocking one of the few schools where there are no problems," Keith said.

Mark regarded his father carefully. Could he hear? Would he? "Dad, there's really something ill with that school," he tried.

His father didn't argue, and that surprised Mark. It was almost as if he didn't want to bother. "Well, you don't rock the boat—especially if you're sitting in it." He stood up from the table. "Let's go. We should be there early."

Mark continued staring at his plate. He didn't stand up. He didn't want to go.

"Now, Mark," Marta said. "It's an important evening for your father. Besides, what have you got to do that's so important?"

There was suspicion in her voice. Did she know?

Mark stood up, scraped his plate, stuck it in the dishwasher, and followed his parents out the door.

"Good evening." Mrs. Creswood's icy, controlled voice floated out over the packed auditorium. She was at the podium. Behind her sat a semicircle of uncomfortable officials, including Mark's father. "On behalf of myself and the staff, I'd like to thank

you all for turning out in such numbers. I congrat-
ulate you for your concern. Now, before we
begin—"

A parent in the rear stood up. "Excuse me, Mrs.
Creswood, could you skip the preliminaries and tell
us just exactly what you're doing about this mess
here?"

Mrs. Creswood smiled. "Well, when I introduce
Mr. Deaver, he'll talk about our new twenty-four-
hour hot line and our—"

"Wait a minute." The parent interrupted again.
"The kids that need the most help, like the ones
with drug problems, don't go in for hot lines!"

No, Mark thought. They just write to me.

"I know kids," another parent said, standing up.
"They just want to grow up happy!"

Four other parents stood up to break into the
interruptions.

"*Please!*" Mrs. Creswood said.

It didn't work.

"Frankly, this radio person is the whole problem.
Are we going to allow this guy to be heard by
anyone who can turn a dial?"

"One at a time!" Mrs. Creswood ordered, but she
was losing the battle.

"Hey, I worked with teenage gangs in the city
and I say we go after this guy!"

"Yeah, remove him permanently!" another
joined in.

Keith stepped up to the podium and took the
microphone. "One at a time," he said loudly.
"You'll all be heard. I promise you—even if I have
to stay here all night."

Mrs. Creswood grabbed the microphone back

from Keith and spoke to him as if he were a rowdy sophomore. "Please, this is my meeting. I know what I'm doing!"

Then Paige Woodward arrived. She came into the auditorium from the rear, wearing a bandaged nose and a black eye like medals of honor. Her presence silenced the crowd—even Mrs. Creswood.

She walked up to the stage, where she had received so many honors, took the microphone into which she'd made so many thank-you speeches, and made the first speech in her life that meant anything to her.

"My name is Paige Woodward and I have something to say to you. People are saying that Harry is 'introducing' bad things and 'encouraging' bad things. Well, it seems to me that these 'bad things' are already here." She rubbed her face, took a deep breath, and continued. "Why don't you listen? He's trying to tell you there's something wrong with this school!"

"What are you talking about?" Mrs. Creswood said derisively.

Paige looked at her principal as if seeing her for the first time. She continued telling her story. "Everybody here is on probation of some kind. It's pathetic. We're all scared to be who we really are. I'm just going through the motions of being perfect, but inside I'm screaming. Can't you hear me?"

"Young lady, I cannot have that Harry defended here. Especially by you!"

"Let her speak!" Keith broke in.

"I will not!" Mrs. Creswood declared. "What we have here is a model student who has been influenced by an outsider. She's going to Yale!"

Paige looked at her in disbelief. She handed the microphone back to Mrs. Creswood. What she had to say next wouldn't need amplification.

"You know what?" she called, marching back out the way she'd come. "You can *all* go to Yale!"

"Paige, Paige! Please come back and speak!" Keith called out after her. The door slammed behind her.

That was all Mark could take. He leaned over to his mother. "I'll meet you guys at home," he said. "I've got tons of homework." He stood up to go.

She tugged at his sleeve. "Mark, I know why you have to get home," she said.

Did she?

"You're planning to listen to that show, aren't you?

Mark shrugged and left.

⊙

Paige pushed through the crowd by the door of the auditorium. Microphones and video cameras threatened to bar her way.

"Are you prepared to do everything he says?" one woman asked.

"Do you know who he is?"

"Are you under psychiatric treatment?"

She couldn't answer all of the questions at once. She didn't want to answer any of them. She grabbed a microphone. Others encroached.

"Are you out there, Harry? Can you hear me? Don't listen to them. Stay on. Stand hard! Talk Hard! Aoughhhhhh!"

Puzzled news reporters watched her walk away toward the baseball field.

A dark-haired girl named Nora something waved at her. "Yo, Paige!" she said, offering her hand for a high five.

Paige slapped the hand and smiled.

⊙

Hundreds of cars filled the baseball field. Students milled everywhere, looking at their watches, checking the tuning on their radios. Two police cars had joined the melee. The students ignored their presence, just as they ignored the video cam crews and the mass of reporters combing the field for anything that could pass as news.

Mazz climbed into his car and turned up the radio, listening to the static, waiting for it to be broken by the mellifluous tones of his man, Harry.

He sat on the back of the driver's seat, visible to anybody looking his way.

"Ten! . . . Nine! . . . Eight! . . . Seven! . . . Six! . . . Five! . . ." the crowd counted in unison. "Four! . . . Three! . . . Two! . . . One!"

Nothing.

Sometimes he was a few minutes late, Mazz reminded himself. Maybe this was one of those times.

Maybe he had a big test tomorrow and couldn't.

Maybe he'd been busted.

Maybe he was afraid.

Mazz began singing the song:

"Everybody knows that the dice are loaded."

Others joined in.

"Everybody rolls with their fingers crossed."

"Come on, Harry, baby. Don't stiff us!"

Maybe he was in the bathroom.

Maybe his clock stopped.

Nora turned off her car radio. He wasn't going to come to her. She would have to go to him.

She got out of the car and walked.

He was there. Behind his house, outside his own sliding door, Mark had a fire going.

"No!" Nora cried, running up to him. Then she saw what he was doing. He was using the family barbecue grill to burn Hard Harry's letters.

"I thought you were—never mind," she said.

He tossed the last letter onto the fire, squirted it with its own dose of fire starter, and walked back into his room. Nora followed.

"Here," she said. "I snuck some messages off the board at the Alcove for you. Thought you might want them."

He stepped back out and tossed them onto the grill without hesitation.

"So, I guess you're not going on tonight, huh?"

"Brilliant," he said.

"You won't believe what's going on out there," she said, pointing in the direction of the school and the baseball field.

Mark laughed, and she didn't know why.

"Hey, is this all a joke to you? You can't just shout 'Fire!' and walk out of a room. That's what you've done, you know, and the fire is burning— booming!"

He looked at her. He seemed to be trying to say something, but she didn't know what, and she had the awful feeling she wasn't going to want to hear it if and when he said it. So she kept on talking.

"You have a responsibility to the people that believe in you. What *is* this anyway? Say something. Say *anything*. Open your mouth up and say, 'Get the hell out of here, *bitch*!' "

"I can't," he uttered.

"You can't what?" she demanded.

"I can't talk!"

This was crazy. "Sure you can talk," Nora said.

"Not to you, I can't," he replied.

The pain on his face was real. Nora didn't understand it, but she knew it.

Then he turned from her, reached for his transmitter, flipped a switch, and brought the mike boom to his lips.

"I got a letter from a person with a problem," he told the mike. Even from his house, Nora could hear the cheers of kids in the baseball field who were receiving his broadcast.

"He couldn't talk. I mean, he could talk, but never when he wanted to. Not to girls. Not to people. He didn't stutter or anything, he just opened up his mouth and nothing came out."

Then Nora understood. This boy who could make love to the world with a microphone couldn't bring himself to say a word to a person he cared about.

Upstairs, Keith and Marta Hunter were returning from the school meeting. Keith turned on the radio as soon as they walked in and found the station where Hard Harry was broadcasting. Marta went to the kitchen to get them something to drink while they listened. She heard something else, though. She heard a voice in the basement, talking loudly.

It was Mark, all right, but it was someone else, too. She knew.

Keith turned up the radio.

*"And this jerk found someone he likes, which is kind of the worst thing that can happen if you can't talk."*

"Keith, come downstairs with me," Marta said.

Keith turned down the volume and followed Marta. Mark's door was locked and bolted. Marta knocked gently.

⊙

"So anyway, I don't know what to tell this guy because lately every time I give advice, the fit hits the shan."

There it was again, the knocking. But his parents were at the meeting. He must be hearing things.

"So, who knows? Maybe the best thing to do is bite the bullet."

"Mark, let us in!" his father's urgent tone was unmistakable.

"Oops!" he said, slamming the switch and silencing his broadcast. He spread his record albums over the transmitter, stuffed his microphone into a drawer, shouted "I'm coming," and let his parents in.

"What were you doing in here?" his father demanded.

Mark pasted an innocent look on his face and shrugged. "My homework," he said.

"Mark, we *heard*. We heard you talking," his mother said insistently.

"He was talking to me," Nora said, standing up

from behind the sofa. Mark wasn't sure whether he or his parents were more surprised.

"Hi, I'm Nora DiNiro. I was afraid you'd be mad at me for interrupting Mark's homework."

Keith gaped for just a second, then recovered. "Oh, not at all," he said.

"You don't know how pleased we are to meet you," Marta said. She offered a hand and Nora shook it.

"Well, I've got to go now," Nora said lightly. "See you!" She slipped out the back door and into the night.

Keith and Marta waved good-bye.

"Mark, why didn't you tell us you had a girl-friend?" Marta asked.

"You devil, you!" his father said, winking before he turned to leave Mark's room. "For a minute we thought *you* were that crazy pirate DJ!"

Keith and Marta laughed. Mark managed a polite smile at the joke.

"Dad, I have something to tell you," he said. His father turned and waited. "Maybe that DJ's not crazy."

Keith shook his head. "Trust me, son, he's crazy. Come on, Marta. I could use a drink. Mark, you want a soda or something?"

"No, thanks."

The door closed. Mark refastened the bolts. He was alone again. He was Harry again. He pulled his shirt off over his head. The cool evening air lifted his troubles.

He brought out his microphone, removed the camouflage from his desk, and switched on his transmitter.

"Sorry about that, folks—technical difficulties."
He breathed deeply. It felt good. In fact, everything
felt good. "So, who have we got out there tonight?
The usual band of Teenage Malcontents? Good,
because Hard Harry's feeling kind of *rude*."

**17**

The electric feeling filled the air at the baseball field as car radios and boom boxes were turned up to full volume. Hard Harry was back home at 92FM.

*"Well, the big news is the emergency PTA meeting to discuss yours truly. All the 'professionals' came out to talk about me. And now they've all run home to tune in and see what they're talking about!"*

Heavy-metal music soared across the field, creating a curtain of noise that baffled interference for Harry's listeners and simply baffled all others.

He spoke again. *"They say I'm deluded, demented, deranged; but guess what I say?"*

Everyone on the baseball field knew the answer to that. They shouted it so their voices echoed off Paradise's hills:

# "SO BE IT!"

Murdock and Mrs. Creswood sat in her office, amid piles of student files to be reviewed, listening intently. They didn't like what they heard.

*"I say death to all vice principals. Why not? Rise up in the cafeteria and stab them with your plastic forks!"*

The color rose in Murdock's face.

*"I say flogging and flagellation for Mrs. Creswood! A hundred lashes for every person she hounded out!"*

Mrs. Creswood didn't blink.

⊙

Mr. Deaver was prepared. He waited in the new 24-hour hot line BIONIC (Believe It or Not, I Care) Headquarters. His radio was tuned to 92FM as well. He knew what was inevitable.

*"Down with all guidance counselors! Make them work for a living. Better yet, make them take guidance counseling!"*

⊙

Mark's eyes lit up. He picked up his cordless phone, checked the scrap of paper where he'd written the "hot line" number, and dialed. It was answered on the first ring.

*"Hot line. Believe It or Not, I Care."*

⊙

The woman in the office clutched the phone to her ear uncertainly. This was new to her. All this equipment. All this excitement. Would she do it right? Her knuckles were white.

*"Hi. Believe it or not, this is Hard Harry and I'd like the pleasure of speaking with Mr. Deaver."*

She nodded—her signal. It was *him.*

"Just a moment. I'll see if he's available." She pressed "hold."

Above her, on the radio, Harry continued talking.

*"I love the thought of Deaver trying to decide if he's available!"*

While Harry chatted and the "hold" button blinked, two police technicians went about their business. Within a few seconds they nodded. They were getting it.

*"Cool. The guy puts me on hold. I love it!"*

Thumbs up. Done.

*"You can run, but you cannot hide, Mr. Deaver!"*

Mr. Deaver picked up the phone, waving good-bye to the police, who scurried out the door as he began speaking.

"Hello, my friend," Deaver said sweetly.

⊙

Mark grinned. There was something wonderfully satisfying about talking to somebody who was such a total ass as his school's guidance counselor.

"You know exactly what I'm talking about, don't you?" he asked accusingly.

Deaver didn't answer the question.

*"It's all over, son,"* he said, obviously trying his best to sound paternalistic. Mark thought he

sounded like a paternalistic ass. *"This call has been traced and, whoever you are, you're finished."*

That's the way it was with technology. You used it, it used you, it abused you. Phone calls could be traced. Mark knew that. He'd always known that.

"Well, so be it," he told Deaver. "Hallelujah!"

He disconnected, and put the cordless phone back on his desk.

"Hallelujah! Hallelujah!" he repeated lazily.

⊙

Mazz leaned forward tensely. He'd seen the cop movies. He knew what it meant when they traced a call. All over the city, cop cars would be putting on their flashing lights. Sirens would blare. Everybody would be closing in on the source of the signal. They'd find *him*. And all he could say was So be it and Hallelujah?

Mazz yelled frantically at the console. "Don't just sit there, man. Run!"

⊙

Mark regarded the mike curiously; held it to his lips; spoke into it.

"I don't know. In the beginning, I was just throwing out thoughts. Throwaway thoughts. For throwaway people." He stood up and walked over to his studio's sliding door. He looked out over the expanse of houses just like his own and found the one he wanted to see, a block and a half away. Police cars surrounded it. Blue, red, and white lights flashed brilliantly in the night. Police-car doors slammed.

"Anyway, what's happening is that the police are busting some poor little old lady who's been unknowingly supplying me with my phone line."

A woman in a bathrobe with curlers in her hair appeared in the driveway of the house. She was hustled into the police car while police invaded her home.

"You see, folks," Mark told his microphone. "I could be anywhere. . . . I *am* anywhere. I'm inside each and every one of you. Yes, just look inside and I'll be in there grinning out at you. Naked!"

He put on a record. Across the street and down the block, the cops emerged from the woman's house, shrugging. Then they figured it out. One policeman followed the overhead wire into her garden shed. That's where Mark had tapped in to borrow her phone line. In a few seconds, his own phone went dead. It didn't matter. They would never find him. The cordless phone reached up to 1,000 yards. They couldn't search every house in that radius. He was okay. He didn't need a phone. He just needed airwaves, and they couldn't take those away from him.

While the music played, he clicked on his television to find out the latest about himself. He turned down the music and talked.

"Just watched the eleven o'clock news. Jesus, they're churning out stuff on me as fast as they can make it up!" he mused. "Turns out they're feeding me 'live' all over the state, but with a delay in case I suddenly mention that Russian poet Who-bitcha Cockoff."

⊙

At the Alcove, the students covered one of Mrs. Creswood's inspirational banners (193 days to SATs) with one of their own,

# DELUDED, DEMENTED, AND DERANGED. SO BE IT!

*"I heard that WBXL is running a phone-in popularity poll. Seems I'm really popular, but I'm getting tired of dialing!"*

⊙

In the baseball field, students danced to every note, hung on every word.

*"Oh, I feel so loved. Seems I'm wanted by the Arizona DA. Not to mention the PTA, the EPA, and the ASPCA! And apparently the FBI are after me because my voice is going across state lines. Speaking of the Feds, anyone listening to me now is accessory to the theft of a valuable government resource: the air!"*

⊙

Mark smiled at his microphone, satisfied. He was on. It was good. They might catch him sometime, but they hadn't gotten him tonight.

He looked at his watch. It was 1:15. "Whoa. Time flies when you're on the run," he said. His mind raced back through the whole evening—the PTA, Nora, his parents, Nora, Mr. Deaver, Nora. "Well, I'm going to cut out now with this unusual song that I'm dedicating to an unusual person I know who makes me feel kind of useless and brainless."

As he spoke, he took a record out of its jacket and put it on his turntable. He cued it to the instrumental he wanted, turned it on, and let it play. The music spoke for him as he couldn't speak for himself. It was slow, deep, sultry, pulsing.

He clicked off his mike and walked to the terrace outside his room. The cool desert night brushed against his bare chest. He breathed deeply, feeling the coolness mingle with his own warmth.

Nora was there. Waiting. She turned down her radio and stood up, walking to him slowly.

"Come to me. Or I'll come to you."

He groped for words. She put her soft finger on his lips.

"That's okay. You don't have to talk," she said.

"Okay," he said.

She stepped closer. So close, he could feel her breath. "You don't have to say anything and you don't have to do anything."

"Okay."

"Unless you want to."

She stood in front of him. All of her was right there. It was the girl he knew from the airwaves, from her poetry, it was the girl he knew from the library, from the stairs, from his own room. But they were all one now—one very unusual person. Nora.

She licked her lips.

He spoke. "We're so different," he tried.

She looked at his bare chest. She didn't hesitate. In one smooth motion, she removed her own sweater.

"Not anymore," she told him, laughing with her eyes.

"No, I meant you're so fearless. I wish I could be like you. I wish I could say things to you."

"You are. You do," she said, reaching.

He took her hands in his. "Everything's so strange," he said.

"Yeah."

"Maybe we're insane," he said.

"So be it."

He pulled her to him, closer, closer. She lifted her arms and encircled his neck. He leaned his face toward hers, reaching for her parted lips with his. He kissed her. She kissed him back, her warmth flowing into him, radiating through him.

A car door slammed. Mark and Nora dropped flat to the ground and peered through blades of grass across the street and down the hill to where they saw a police car. Nora turned to him with fear in her eyes.

He shook his head. "They're just bringing back the lady whose phone I've been using. They won't find me that way. They won't find us." He held her closely, never wanting the moment to stop. He reached to kiss her again. She tickled him. He laughed. They smiled.

Mark felt comfortable, warm, happy, at ease. At that moment, nothing else in the world mattered to him except himself and Nora.

She felt it, too. He knew she did. Her eyes sparkled, reflecting his own joy.

And then, it was almost too much. It was immense and precarious and overwhelming. It was terrifying.

"Let's take a break for station identification," Nora said, reaching for her sweater. She slipped it back on.

They stood up. He touched her face. She kissed him on the lips.

She was gone.

**18**

When Mark arrived at school the next morning, he found two things that made him uncomfortably aware of how fast his universe was changing.

First he found Shep Sheppard Reporting standing by the entrance, talking to a camera.

"It's been three days since the death of Malcolm Kaiser and state and local officials still have little idea of the identity of the so-called Hard Harry. Although many are convinced he is a student at this school. Perhaps he's one of the students you see entering the school at this very moment."

Shep gestured grandly toward all the students milling in front of the building. Mark felt as if he were pointing directly at him.

Nora was there, too, standing quietly by the door. She took up his pace as he passed her, and they walked toward the Alcove together, not touching, not speaking, but completely bound together.

In the Alcove, they found the usual milling students, the usual music playing, and an unusual collection of messages on the message board. Cautiously, hoping not to draw attention, they read some of the hundreds of cards pinned there for Hard Harry. They drew no attention at all. Everybody else was reading them, too.

"This is deep! Your message is *out* there!" Nora said, the excitement rising in her voice.

"But I don't have a message," Mark protested.

"Sure you do," Nora said.

He could feel his own fears growing again. He couldn't understand how anybody could care what he had to say. And how was he supposed to handle what other people cared about when he couldn't handle what *he* cared about.

"This whole thing is making me ill," he said.

Nora led him to a quiet corner where they could talk.

"What's wrong with you?" she asked.

Mark was shaking with terror. "Last night was a mistake. I'm not going on anymore."

"But you're so close."

"Close to what?" he asked, exasperated.

"Getting your message out!"

Mark stared at her. She didn't understand at all. She wasn't afraid of anything. "Wait. This is my life you're playing with."

"Not anymore it isn't. It's everyone's life."

She was right and he knew it and he hated her for being right. Why couldn't it be like it was? Why couldn't he just go on talking to a microphone, ragging people who badly needed to be ragged? Why did he have to have a message? Why did it have to have an answer?

He turned to go. Nora grabbed his arm and turned him to her.

"You can't leave it like this. Everyone's confused."

"So am I. This is fucked up!"

Nora looked at him. "No, the world is fucked up! Just like you said. Mark, don't you see, you're the voice. You're the voice you were waiting for!"

The voice? The voice everybody wanted to hear was made by a voice harmonizer that disguised the sound of his voice from everybody. It was a phony just like he was. How could Nora believe in that?

"You're completely nuts," he said. He walked away.

When he turned around to apologize, she wasn't there.

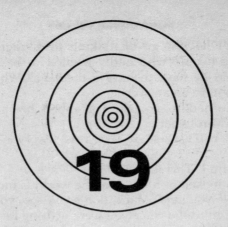

**19**

"Yeah, well you make me nuts," Nora muttered to Mark's retreating back.

"Mrs. Creswood wants to see you," Murdock said, pulling at Nora's arm. She reacted automatically, jerking it back from him. "And you, and you, and you," he said, pointing to Donald, Janie, and Holden. Two others were already trailing him.

"What are we being arrested for?" Nora demanded.

Murdock smirked. "We'll see when we look at your files."

Mrs. Creswood was on the phone when they got to her office. The six students were seated in a row in front of her desk while she finished her call.

"No, Keith. Everything is under control. I've just ordered psychiatric evaluations for a couple of the key troublemakers and I've— I can do whatever I like. It's *my* school, Commissioner. . . . No, you're not coming over here. You'll only upset things more. Good-bye."

Nora thought she heard Murdock gasp a little, but before she could investigate, Mrs. Creswood's palms slapped onto a pile of files on her desk. She leaned forward and moved her piercing eyes slowly along the line of students. When she had finished glaring, she spoke.

"Shall we have a look at these files or shall we discuss the identity of our DJ friend?" she asked menacingly.

Next to her, Nora could feel Holden shudder.

$\odot$

Lunchtime. For the first time all year, Mark was relieved to hear it. He had to find Nora. She hadn't been in class all morning. She hadn't been near her locker; she wasn't in the library; she wasn't hiding out in the art room. He had to talk to her. But first, he had to find her.

Mark tried the Alcove. Things were really popping there. Masses of students had come to see, to read, to leave messages, to talk to others, to speculate. It seemed to Mark that everybody was there but Nora.

Murdock, Deaver, and another teacher were patrolling nervously, glancing this way and that. Mark wondered what they expected to happen. Whatever it was, they obviously planned to be ready. Deaver slapped at his leg with a metal ruler. Murdock had his whistle clenched in his teeth.

Suddenly, music blasted into the air.

"Everybody knows that the dice are loaded.

Everybody knows—"

It only took Murdock a second to silence the machine, but it was swept out of his reach by one of the students. Another began singing the song without playing it. Others joined it.

Murdock dropped the whistle from his teeth. It dangled on the lanyard, bouncing on his barrel chest as he spoke loudly. "Don't push me, people!" Murdock threatened.

"Aoughhhhhh!"

Mr. Deaver glared. Murdock made a note on the pad on his clipboard.

Cheryl Biggs emerged from the crowd. "Hi, Mr. Deaver!" she said brightly. In her hand she had a white four-by-six card. She waved it in front of him, then spoke to the students. "They got forced to take me back, see?"

Mr. Deaver's lips thinned to a narrow line.

Mark watched as attention shifted to a newcomer. A kid with short-cropped bleached hair and four earrings in one ear worked his way through the crowd to the bulletin board at the rear of the Alcove. He was carrying a sheet of paper—a message. This was another one of his listeners.

Murdock blocked the kid's way.

"I'm putting this up and no one's stopping me."

"You're not a student here anymore, Mazzilli," Murdock said.

"What's happening, Einstein?" the kid retorted. "Is that your face or did your neck throw up?"

Murdock grabbed for the boy's neck.

"Go ahead. Slam me. That's all you're good for!"

Murdock dropped his clipboard, drew back his left arm, and swung. Mark couldn't watch anymore. He fled.

⊙

Jan Emerson heard a commotion and ran to the Alcove. Mr. Deaver was tugging at Murdock, trying to pull him off a student whom he was pummeling, systematically, repeatedly.

"Stop! That's enough! What's wrong with you?" she said, grabbing Murdock's arm. Together, she and Mr. Deaver succeeded in pulling him away from the student just in time for Mrs. Creswood's arrival. For once Jan welcomed the woman's presence.

"Jesus, he was beating a student!" Jan said. "What's wrong with this school?"

"Control yourself, Miss Emerson."

Jan was stunned. "*Me?* Control myself? I will not—"

"Or suffer the consequences."

Jan stared at Mrs. Creswood in disbelief. "What are you talking about?" she asked.

"I'm talking about your dismissal," Mrs. Creswood said coolly. "You may leave now."

Jan stood and stared for a moment—just long enough to see Mazz take advantage of the quiet to put his message on the board for Harry. It read:

# I GOT A RIGHT TO A EDUCATION.

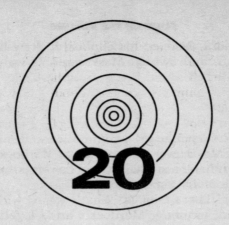

# 20

There was Nora, finally. She was standing by her
locker, looking distraught. Talking was hard, apol-
ogizing was harder, but Nora was important. Mark
hurried to her.

"I've been looking all over for you," he began.

"Forget it. Look," she said, pointing to the baseball field.

Three yellow panel trucks were parked in the
outfield. In bold capital letters, they proclaimed
their business. FCC.

"Yeah, I know. Federal Communications Commission. Sure, with those trucks, they can drive
around and triangulate where a radio signal is
coming from."

It was the end. He knew it. He had felt it would
come.

Nora did, too. "So to hell with it. It's over. And, frankly, I don't even care anymore."

That didn't sound like Nora. Where was the girl who was going to tell him about his voice, his message.

"What's up?" he asked, noticing for the first time that she seemed to be cleaning out her locker.

"I just got expelled," she said.

"Why? You're smart. You've won prizes in art and all kinds of stuff."

"I'm failing math," she explained.

"They can't kick you out for that."

"Says in my file I've been cutting classes and I'm way over the limit, but they didn't tell me until now."

"That's just a suspension," Mark said.

Nora allowed herself a little smile. "Then I said 'Fuck you!' to Creswood. You should have seen her face. She was so happy for the excuse to expel me she even thanked me!"

"I *hate* this school!" Mark said.

"Correct. And that's why I don't care about being kicked out. Besides, it was worth it to tell Creswood off." She slammed her locker closed. "Bye. It was fun while it lasted."

"Wait!" he called.

"Forget it," she said. "There's nothing you can do about it."

She turned to go.

Mark started to follow her, but somebody else called to him. It was Miss Emerson. Something in her face made him stop.

"I'm leaving the school," she said. "I just wanted to tell you good-bye and good luck."

Mark suddenly had the feeling that everybody who mattered was leaving the school at the same time and that it was all because of him.

"Why?" he asked.

"I was fired. Seems I don't fit in around here," she explained. "It was my mistake to think I could change things. You don't rock the boat—" she began.

"Especially when you're sitting in it," he finished for her. His father's favorite expression came bitingly off his tongue.

Miss Emerson nodded knowingly. "Chin up. Look after yourself. You're good, you know."

"Thanks," he said. He watched her walk back toward the parking lot and then, apparently changing her mind, turning in to the door marked Admin/Records.

For his own part, Mark was beginning to get a hankering for the open sea in a rocky boat.

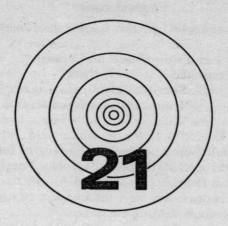

**21**

Mark glanced at the television. Once again he was the news. This time, a Mr. Arthur Watt of the FCC was talking.

*"Good evening,"* he said pompously to the camera. *"Rumors and falsehoods notwithstanding, we at the FCC feel that Democracy is all about protecting the privacy of the ordinary citizen. Unregulated radio would result in programming by the lowest common denominator—the rule of the mob."*

The lowest common denominator unplugged his transmitter and sorted through his tapes, dropping a few into a carton nearby.

*"This is vandalism, not free expression. We know he's in the neighborhood. One more transmission, and we'll get him."*

Mark snapped off the television. Enough was enough.

He picked up the phone and dialed the number he'd memorized. "Is Nora there?" he asked. No. "Could you tell her that Mark called again?"

He hung up and returned his attention to his tapes.

Near the school, the baseball field was completely filled up, allowing only a narrow lane that had been roped off for the FCC trucks. Nearly every student in the school was there. All the car radios and the boom boxes were tuned and ready, waiting for ten o'clock, waiting for Harry.

In equal number to the students were the reporters, newscasters, techies, and hangers-on. Some reporters searched frantically for another student to interview. Another paid Donald ten dollars per tape as fast as he could churn them out.

⊙

In the school, a meeting was in progress.

"What's going on in this school?" Keith demanded. "I'm seeing a lot of turmoil and unhappiness."

"It's the troublemakers," Mrs. Creswood said without emotion. "You can't run a top school with troublemakers in the mix."

"But what exactly *is* a troublemaker, Loretta?" Keith asked, aware that he was the first person he had ever heard call her by her first name.

"Someone who has no interest in education," she answered promptly.

It was getting bizarre. "That's practically every

teenager, isn't it?" he asked, chuckling. Others laughed audibly.

Loretta Creswood would not be made to appear ridiculous. "Can't you understand that nothing is more important than a good education?" she asked.

"Except the basic right to it," Keith said softly.

"The point is, I have the highest average SAT scores in the state," Mrs. Creswood said with pride.

"Apparently by sacrificing the slower students," Keith countered.

"I stand by my record."

The room was quiet. The meeting adjourned.

⊙

Mark was nearly finished. His desk was empty. There was no sign of his microphone or his broadcast equipment. His tapes were stowed, his harmonizer, too. It was a quarter of ten.

⊙

On the baseball field, the carnival continued. Students in weird costumes danced to Hard Harry's tapes while FCC minions measured everything they could think of. Mazz Mazzilli carried a boom box with him, climbing on top of Arthur Watt's stretch limo where he was joined by Paige Woodward, wearing Yale blue—and shocking pink.

⊙

Nora was in her room. There was no point in waiting at the baseball field; there was nothing to wait for. There was no reason to go to Mark's house; there was no one to go for. She just sat, looking at the bare walls and the pile of pictures and clothes she'd removed from them.

Her radio was tuned to 92FM—just in case. But it only gave out a hum.

"Nora, you okay?"

She looked up. There, coming into her open window, was Mark Hunter.

"Yeah, I'm okay, I'm fine," she said. "I just didn't think we needed to talk anymore."

"I need your help," he said.

"No, you don't," she answered automatically. She didn't want to get involved, to care for somebody who wasn't going to care back.

"I do," Mark said. "I started something here, and I have to finish it."

"You mean it?"

"Yeah, look at this," he said, leading her to her own window.

She looked out. There, parked next to her house, was, at first glance, a Jeep. At second glance, it was a portable radio station.

Nora followed Mark out the window and examined the setup. There were a dozen automobile batteries attached to Mark's transmitter, his synthesizer, his tape deck, and his microphone. A ten-foot antenna sprouted from the rear of the car.

"Who did all this?"

"Me and Radio Shack," he said. "It's my mom's Jeep. She knows. She's cool."

Nora knew what he wanted her to do. She had to pilot the world's only mobile radio station. A signal that was in constant motion couldn't be triangulated by the FCC or anyone else. She hopped in behind the wheel, reached for the keys, turned on the motor, and gunned the engine. It roared.

"Have you ever driven a Jeep before?" Mark asked dubiously.

Nora shrugged. "Have you ever been broadcast nationally before?" she replied. She shifted into gear and the car lurched forward.

⊙

Click. Hummmmm.

*"Hello Dad? I'm in jail!*

*Hi Dad! I'm in jail! Say hi to Mom!"*

"Aoughhhhhh!" Harry's fans yowled with delight when they heard the broadcast begin. Nobody, nobody but Harry would play that song tonight!

Engines revved in the FCC trucks.

"See you soon!" Watt said, waving good-bye to them.

*"Hi, folks, seems we've got a new listener tonight. He's Mr. Watt of the FCC. Hi, Arthur, thanks for coming out."*

Watt smiled good-naturedly. He'd expected as much. He winked at a nearby news camera. "Thank *you* for coming out," he said with feeling.

*"For those of you who don't know, Watt is just a political hack who got appointed to his job for being the pollster for the president in the last election."*

Watt hadn't expected that. He hoped the trucks got there fast.

*"Imagine a stupid vote counter being in charge of free speech in America. Watt was the guy in high*

*school who took names when the teacher was absent.
He's the guy in politics who wears a wig."*

"This is the problem with free speech," Watt
muttered, and then escaped to the luxurious quiet
of his limo.

⊙

The Jeep swerved to the left, along a dirt road
that led to the desert preserve behind the school.
In her rearview mirror Nora saw two yellow trucks
nearly collide at the intersection they'd crossed
only seconds before.

Next to her, Mark was shuffling papers. The music ended. He spoke.

"Maybe somebody can explain the mysterious
disappearance of Luis Chavez—age fifteen and giving up. Legally kicked out on September 26th.
Arthur Washington, age sixteen. Expelled on September 27th. Hector Garcia, age fourteen. Trans-
ferred to Special Ed on October 1st. Garcia, Garvey,
Gomez, Hansen, Kunsler . . ."

⊙

Keith listened. *"Lamont, Larraby, Lopez, Mac-
Donald, Mazzilli . . ."* He looked at Mrs. Creswood
curiously.

"So what does *this* prove?" she asked defensively.
"Not everyone goes to college."

Jan Emerson arrived. She was holding a school
record folder in her hand.

"Mr. Hunter," she said, almost breathless because she had been running, looking everywhere
for him. "I think you should be aware of something." She handed him the file. "Look, this is Luis
Chavez's file. He's gone, but the government money

to educate him isn't. After she gets the money for each kid enrolled, she starts purging the enrollment—one at a time."

"This woman is no longer employed here," Mrs. Creswood said, pointing to Jan. Her voice cracked with outrage.

"—and only the dumb ones. And only the defenseless ones."

"Nonsense!" Mrs. Creswood huffed. "This woman doesn't know what she's talking about."

Jan turned to face the principal. "In the first week of school, you flagged all the names with low SAT scores and started files on them. Why?"

"What are you doing on school property?" Mrs. Creswood countered unsuccessfully.

"Why?" Jan persisted. "For extra tutoring?" she asked sarcastically.

Keith looked at the file Jan had given him. "It seems these kids are still on the rolls," he said.

"The money went to the school," Mrs. Creswood said, trying to defend herself.

"Those kids had rights," Jan said.

"They were losers," Mrs. Creswood said.

Keith had seen enough. "It's fascist, racist, and criminal behavior on your part and I'm suspending you."

"You can't do that!"

"I just did."

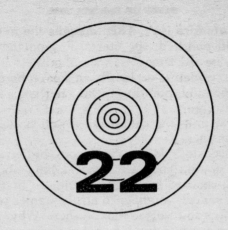

# 22

Mark barely saw the countryside that flew by, he didn't feel the wind, taste the dust, hear the squeal of the Jeep's tires, or smell the cool evening. He only knew that Nora was next to him, and the microphone was in his hands.

"People say my ideas are dangerous. Well, that's bull because there's no such thing as a dangerous idea. There are only stupid and smart ideas. Like when I suggest suicide is thinkable, suddenly I'm not allowed to say that. Suddenly I'm out of control. Suddenly, I'm irresponsible and dangerous. Well, I say they are dangerous!"

Nora spotted a yellow truck ahead. She made a U-turn—at fifty miles an hour.

"Yeah, welcome to Radio Free America! We're

ready. America is ready for a million voices crying out in the wilderness!"

Nora turned off her lights and pulled into a cul-de-sac. The yellow truck whizzed past. Nora jerked the Jeep into reverse, flipped on the lights, and pulled out, turning in the opposite direction.

The Jeep slapped through a pothole. Nora and Mark both bounced eight inches out of their seats and landed hard. Mark's harmonizer flew out of his hands, slammed against the transmitter, and broke into two pieces.

"No!" Mark said. Nora pulled off the road, behind some underbrush, and braked to a halt. Mark looked at the two pieces despairingly. "I need this!" he said.

Nora took the two pieces from his hand and examined them. "Maybe I can fix it," she said. "Give me a minute." She tried to work the pieces together, using the steering wheel for leverage. Nothing could be allowed to stop them: not Creswood, Watt, or the FCC. She was damned if some broken gizmo would do it either. She worked frantically.

The pieces clicked together.

Mark reached for the microphone. He was going to talk without the harmonizer.

"No, wait," she said. "Here!"

He shook his head and switched his mike on. "Okay, people. This is really me now and there are just a few more things I want to say to you all. High school is the bottom. Being a teenager really sucks, but surviving it is the point."

Nora tossed the harmonizer to the back of the Jeep, shifted back into gear, and hit the pedal.

"Things can change, and so can you. Quitting won't make you strong. Living will. So hang on and hang in!"

⊙

On the baseball field, students, police, technicians, and reporters all listened, in rapt attention.

*"What I want is a healing of some kind. Hey, I know all about hating and sneering. I'm the 'why bother' generation. But why did I come out here tonight? And why did you?*

*"Because we want a healing to occur.*

*"I believe with everything that is in me that the whole world is longing for a healing—even the trees and the earth itself are crying out for it. You can hear it everywhere."*

⊙

Nora tore along the road, aware now that the end was inevitable. They were moving all right. They were moving as fast as they could. But the trucks were moving, too, and sooner or later the trucks would find them. Eventually there would be no place to hide.

She turned toward the school. At the very least, they could have the home field advantage.

"Yeah, we're ready. American's ready for a million voices. Maybe mine, maybe yours. Be heard!"

Nora looked at Mark. He looked at her. She was proud of him; he, grateful to her. They had shared

something very precious and there was nothing
that could change that—not even an FCC truck.

"Okay," he said to her unasked question.

Nora turned onto another winding road through
the desert preserve, aware now that there were two
trucks in their wake. If they were going to tail her,
she was going to take them for a ride they'd never
forget!

She swerved up over a rise at the edge of the
road, gunned the motor, and flew across an arid
arroyo, dropping three feet below the other side of
it. Immediately she turned to the right, settling
into a lower roadway. One FCC truck made it. The
other didn't. Nora looked in her rearview mirror.
The yellow truck hung lamely, half in and half out
of the arroyo, spinning its wheels.

She pointed at it and Mark. He laughed.

Nora led the other truck through the backroads
of her childhood, bouncing around the rough ter-
rain of the Arizona desert.

Two more turns, a sharp drop, and they approached the baseball field.

Mark wasn't prepared for the sight that greeted
him. The entire field was filled with cars. They all
had their lights on; they all had their radios blasting. His schoolmates, his listeners, were everywhere, dancing to the music he was playing for
them from the back of his mother's Jeep.

At first, one student saw the Jeep. Then others
spotted it as well, as it descended the final hill and
drove onto the baseball field. They understood. He
had come to them. By the time Mark and Nora hit
the warning track, a thousand students were yell-
ing at them. Horns honked, listeners cheered.

Nora slowed the car and drove majestically down the aisle left for the FCC trucks' escape.

Mark stood up, mike in hand, and spoke.

"One more thing. It's not over yet! Go to Radio Shack! Buy a cheap amplifier. Make an antenna out of coat hangers if you have to. Find a closet, close the door, pick a name, and go on the air.

"Keep this thing going!"

The students cheered. Mark was only vaguely aware of the arrival of Watt, the approach of three police cars.

"I'm calling for every kid out there to seize the air. You're not stealing it! It belongs to you. They can't stop you. Spill your guts out. Say shit and fuck a million times if you want to. *You* decide!"

Nora killed the engine and waited. Six policemen came to the door of the Jeep.

"Don't be sad, be *bad*. Be mad and glad!"

"Right on, my man!"

"Fill the air! Keep it alive!"

And then it died. Watt himself took hold of Mark's antenna and yanked it from the back of the Jeep. The radios in the ball field were silenced. The students were not. They shouted and screamed, filling the night with Harry's "Aoughhhhhh!" Mark knew, as he had never known anything before, that what he had started was right, and that it would go on.

Slowly, deliberately, police handcuffed Mark and Nora and led them out of the Jeep. Mark had never felt better, more alive, in his whole life. He looked at Nora and could feel that she was sharing his moment.

Side by side Mark and Nora crossed the field,

side by side they approached the waiting police van.

Reporters and newscasters pushed to get close to them. "Why did you give up?" one called. "What did you mean by a healing?" another asked. Side by side, they went up the steps and through the double doors of the police van.

"Do you have anything to say?" came the final question.

Mark turned. The policeman at the door of the van held it open. He could see the crowd. He spoke to them.

"Yeah, I have one more thing to say."

His listeners waited.

"Talk hard!"

The cheers were so loud that Mark couldn't even hear the doors slamming.

# THE
# BEGINNING

**23**

"Hi, it's Mad Marie on 86FM in Tucson and my show is *Talk to Me*."

"Mad at the world? Join Jolly Jerry James broadcasting from Arcadia, Maine."

"This is Martin McMartin and my show is called *Turn on Truth*."

"This is Seek and Destroy, coming to you all from Newark, N.J."

"Hi, this is Miss Maligned, and my
show is . . ."

"Tune in with me to
Fly by Night, at . . ."

> ". . . in Daytona, called
> *Air Play* . . ."

"This is *Word Power* on FM . . ."

"This is *Night Talking* . . ."

"It's Pirate at Work . . ."

". . . *Mind over Matter* . . ."

> ". . . Hear Me Out . . ."